A GIFT OF DEATH

DANIEL J. VOLPE

D & T
PUBLISHING

To the band, Everwar. Rock on and melt faces.

TABLE OF CONTENTS

A ROSE OF RED AND WHITE

TRINA'S EARS felt like they were about to bleed. The pressure in her head was building, each thump of the industrial-sized subwoofers assaulting her. She loved every second of it.

Sweaty bodies, mostly clad in black, pushed against her. She pushed back, the beat and violence of the thrash metal fueling her aggression.

She wasn't tall, just barely over five feet, but she could hold her own in any mosh pit. Her fist swung, striking anonymous flesh. There were no apologies in the pit, only chaos and the love of music. There were rules, even though it looked like obscene chaos. Anyone who went down in the pit was helped up immediately, usually, the participants would clear an area for the person. Anyone not wanting to be in the pit was usually left alone unless they were doing hit and runs and then they were fair game. If you jumped in the pit, took a few cheap shots, and jumped out, all bets were off. Gender, age, race, religion didn't mean shit when the music was raging and fists and feet were flying.

Trina had a little buzz on, plus she'd smoked a joint before coming into the show. She felt great. The alcohol and weed made her feel like she was in the matrix. She felt a hot body collide with hers, propelling her forward. She took the gift of momentum, using it to unload a spinning punch, which hit nothing but air.

The violent music, unintelligible lyrics, and the sound of someone raping a guitar slowed down. The guitar wound down, slowing to silence.

Trina watched the mosh pit do the same, the battle ending with the song. Battered, red, and sweating faces looked around at their fellow combatants. Handshakes and back pats were plenty, as was customary after a solid pit. They looked up at the band, a thrash metal group dressed in clown masks and shirtless. Each member was slick with sweat, which dripped from the cheap Halloween masks. Even the singer wore one, which didn't matter because most of the lyrics were screaming anyway.

Trina melted back into the crowd, away from the stage. She was hot. Her back and breasts were drenched and she needed some air. Pushing through a sea of smelly concertgoers, she navigated her way to the back door of the venue.

The cool night air washed over her, embracing her intoxicated skin, licking at the sweat. She was thankful she'd decided to wear her *Everwar* tank top, or else she'd be a puddle. Trina reached into her cleavage, which was ample, and pulled out her cell phone.

Her best friend and concert mate, Kathy, bailed on her at the last minute. There was no way she was missing this concert. Her favorite band, *Shit Fist* was getting their first headline and she had to be there. Besides, she thought the lead singer, Billy Silver, was hot. Trina checked her phone, seeing if maybe Kathy was feeling better and would make it out, but her messages were blank.

"Your loss," she said to herself, replacing her phone and grabbing a pack of cigarettes. Luckily for her, her cleavage was a perfect storage spot. Her pants took 20 minutes to get on and the pockets were so tight she could barely get money in them. She didn't care. They made her ass look great. Trina leaned against a chain-link fence smoking her cigarette. More sweaty smokers stepped out, joining the growing group. Some even smoked a little weed, a risk knowing they could get thrown out. She wished she was brave enough to puff off the roach clip she had in the cigarette pack, but she wasn't. She couldn't get tossed out before seeing Billy perform.

Trina wandered around the small fenced-in smoking area, looking for a place to toss her butt. The parking lot was behind the fence and she noticed an odd vehicle. One she hadn't seen when she pulled in.

It was a camper, but not an ordinary one. No, this one was painted black and had the letters 'AGOD' painted in red along the side. Exhaust smoke was drifting out of the tailpipe, winding into the night air. Trina stared at the odd-looking RV for a moment longer before tossing her cigarette onto the ground.

She walked back into the venue, the smell and heat assaulting her senses. She was sweaty too but hoped she didn't smell too bad. She brushed her dyed, black hair behind her ear, dozens of bracelets jingling as she did.

"Alright, motherfuckers," the MC said, grabbing the mic. The curtain behind him was closed, giving the masked band time to remove their equipment and allow the next band to set up. "We have a real treat for you tonight," some of the crowd was paying attention, but most were stacked up at the bar trying to get a drink before the next act started. "An unexpected band was a late edition, but I think they're going to melt your fucking faces!" He yelled into the mic, a whine of feedback garnered boos from the crowd. The MC, who was as pale as a ghost, blushed, his red cheeks standing out against his black clothes. "Fuck you," he said, flipping the bird to the crowd. They all laughed at him but started moving back towards the stage, anxious for some new metal. A stagehand came out from the curtains. The MC covered the mic, talking with the heavyset woman, who had a headset on. Her chins shook as she spoke. The MC nodded and the stagehand waddled away. "Alright, cocksuckers, without further ado, I give you your next band." He paused for dramatics, but the audience was already drunk and fired up. They did not need theatrics. "*A Gift of Death*." He growled the last part as the curtains opened in blackness.

Trina watched, seeing silhouettes moving in the shadows. Dim safety lights behind the stage gave a little glimpse, but nothing more than a tease. She moved her way closer and noticed at least one of the band members was a female. It wasn't just the long hair that gave it away, fuck most guys in metal have long hair. No, it was the curvy ass and nice set of tits. They weren't as big as hers, but they were certainly enough.

The curvy woman approached the mic, her black hair covering her face like the girl from *The Ring*. A bass guitar was dangling from her neck and she reached up, stroking the mic with fish netted hands. Red lights lit the stage and a guitar whined a note, holding it until the crowd looked at them on stage.

She flipped her hair back and Trina was in awe. Before her stood the pinnacle of a goth hottie. Average height, large tits, tight waist, black hair, and piercings gleaming on her face.

Trina was far from a lesbian, even though her first sexual experience was in middle school when her best friend, Jannet, fingered her after a softball game. Even though Trina loved men, she couldn't help thinking unsavory thoughts about the woman on stage.

"Hello Newburgh!" the woman said, gripping the mic.

The crowd, still unsure of this new band, cheered, but not nearly as loud as before.

The woman looked to the two other band members; another

female, this one with a guitar around her neck, and a male, who sat behind an impressive set of drums.

"Ok, motherfuckers," she said into the mic, her predatory eyes scanning the crowd.

People fell silent when those dark eyes passed over them. Except for Trina. She felt a flutter when they locked with hers. It may have been nothing, but she could've sworn they lingered on her for just a moment longer.

"Vee," she said to the guitar player, "give'em a taste."

Vee was tall. Much taller than an average woman. She wore a thin tank top and had no bra on; her hard nipples pressed against the fabric. Her hair was dyed fluorescent green and cut short and spiky. Her eyes were sunken and she had a heroin chic look about her.

Vee's fingers, holding a pick made of bone, flew over the strings. They hummed a violent sound. The crowd began to come alive as the last note dwindled. Grumbles of approval floated through the air.

"Nic," the woman on the mic said, not looking back at her drummer.

Nic began a slow beat of the bass drum before coming alive. The fury and speed of his double bass shook the walls and rattled chests.

"Huh, I guess that leaves me," she said. The crowd was cheering and whistling. The woman, clad in black, began stroking her bass guitar. Deep, melodious sounds poured over the crowd, who was cheering in earnest now.

Trina felt electrified. Her arms were covered in goosebumps as she stared at the goddess behind the mic. Again, they locked eyes, this time the woman smiled, just a little, but enough to let her know.

"Alright, you heaps of shit. Are you ready for some fucking metal?"

The crowd screamed, pushing forward towards the stage. Trina, caught in the wave of bodies, was feet from the stage.

"We are *A Gift of Death* and we're here to blow your fucking minds!" she slid her fingers down the strings of her bass. "I'm Sarin." She put a black finger-nailed hand on her chest. "That hot bitch over there is Vee-Exx." The green-haired guitar player hit a few strings. "And that hot piece of meat on the drums is Arsenic, but we just call him Nic." On cue, Nic built up a symbol strike ending with a hard hit.

By now the crowd was electric. Everyone was packed in front of the stage.

Trina couldn't stop looking at Sarin. They locked eyes once again and before Sarin belted out her first lyrics, Trina questioned her sexuality in earnest.

THE FINAL ACT had gone off without a hitch. *Shit Fist* played their set and Billy Silver was sober enough to finish the show, which was a small miracle.

Trina hugged herself as she walked through the parking lot looking for her car. She left her hoodie on the passenger seat, knowing there was no place to put it in the venue.

Her ears were still ringing, but she loved it. She didn't know how people wore earplugs during a show. You could still hear the music, but it wasn't the same. It was like sex with a condom; it was better than no sex, but not as good.

The black camper was parked under a street lamp, just in front of her car.

Trina slowed down, hoping to catch a glimpse of Sarin, but the windows were all dark. She did see the drummer, Nic, standing outside smoking a cigarette.

He was scrolling away on his phone, laughing at something before looking up.

Trina thought he was attractive, as most women would. He was of average height and thin. Not sickly thin, but athletic thin, with a swimmer's body. He wore an obscure band shirt, black of course, and his dark hair was slicked back. He had a light beard and coal-black eyes.

Yes, Trina would jump his bones in a heartbeat, but she couldn't get her mind off Sarin. There was something about the way she moved her hips when she sang. The emotion, the rawness of it. Like an open wound, weeping blood, she was exposed. There was a quality about her Trina couldn't ignore. Something carnal called to her and just thinking about the other woman made her pussy hot.

"Hey," Nic said, slipping his phone into his pocket. He took a drag off his cigarette and flicked it. A shower of sparks marked its final resting spot.

Trina stopped, her hands still on her cold, exposed arms. She looked around, figuring he was talking to someone else.

"Yeah, you," Nic said, walking closer. He stopped in front of her. He had both hands in his pockets and a sly grin on his face.

That grin, Trina knew, had taken many girls out of their panties.

"Sarin took a liking to you," he said, pulling a pack of smokes from his pocket. He took one out, lit it, and offered the pack to Trina.

They weren't her brand, but she was out, so it didn't matter.

"Thanks," she said, taking a cigarette.

Nic leaned in with his lighter.

She breathed in fire, lighting her cigarette and blowing blue smoke into the night air. She puffed away, trying to comprehend what he just said to her.

"Me?" she asked, her hand going to her chest and cigarette to her mouth.

Nic smiled, a cloud of smoke flowing from his mouth like

water. "Yeah, well she said and I quote, 'the goth-looking chick with the huge tits and wide eyes' end quote." He smirked.

Trina blushed, smoking to avoid speaking. So, the eye contact was intentional.

"You wanna come in for a drink? Meet the gals?" Nic asked, already walking back to the camper.

Trina was torn. Of course, she wanted to meet them. Their music was amazing and they seemed like a fun bunch to hang with. She also knew she had to work the next day, which was quickly approaching. Kathy was always her voice of reason and she bailed, so Trina knew what to do.

"Sure, I'd love to meet everyone," Trina said, following Nic.

"Great," Nic said, reaching the steps of the camper. He opened the door. "Come on in," he walked through the threshold, inviting her to follow.

The camper was small, but that was to be expected. Trina entered the kitchen/living room, where Nic had opened a small refrigerator. His tight ass was facing her and she wondered if she might be able to get all of them in one bed. She'd never had a threesome, let alone a foursome, but for whatever reason, it seemed like a logical idea.

"Take a seat," he said, pointing to the fold-down table on the wall.

Trina slid into the tight seat. It was cold in the camper, much more than she'd expected. She still rubbed herself for warmth.

"Where is Sarin and…" the name of the green-haired guitar player escaped her.

"Vee-Exx?" Nic said, walking towards her with two glasses in hand. He set one in front of her.

"Yeah, Vee," she said, looking at the drink. She wasn't sure if drinking more was the best idea, but she didn't want to offend her host. She picked up the plastic cup and sipped. The drink was bitter but full of alcohol. *Vodka*, she thought, but it didn't matter. She took another sip, this one bigger than the last.

"This is pretty good," she said, taking a gulp.

Nic watched her, taking conservative sips of his. "I'm glad you think so."

A door on the far side of the camper opened. Trina turned her head and saw Vee and Sarin emerge from a bedroom. The room was small and completely dominated by a black-sheeted bed.

"Ah, you found her," said Sarin, taking Nic's cup from him. "Leave us." She said, putting it to her lips, her dark eyes boring into his. "We have girl-talk to discuss."

Nic looked dejected but listened to Sarin without argument.

'Boss bitch,' Trina thought, taking another drink. The night was catching up to her and she was feeling it. Between the drinks she had in the venue, the weed, and this drink, her mind was starting to wander.

Vee walked past her, still wearing the tank-top. Her small, perky breasts jiggled just slightly as she moved to the fridge. She bent over and Trina could see up her shirt. The woman's nipples were hard, her breasts hanging free. Vee grabbed a beer, opened it, and walked back by Sarin and Trina.

Sarin slid in next to Trina, who was almost finished with her drink.

Trina was on Cloud-9. Her head was swimming and she felt more fucked up than she should.

Sarin grinned at Vee; her lips coated in black lipstick. She then smiled at Trina, who was nodding off.

"So, what did you think of the show?" Sarin asked, putting her hand on Trina's thigh.

Vee slithered into the seat across from them. She put the beer to her lips but didn't drink. Her eyes glued to Sarin. Her free hand rubbed her ever-swelling clit through her pants.

Trina was good and fucked up. Whatever kind of booze was in the drink had her gone.

"Are we moving?" Trina asked, looking towards the curtained off driver's seat.

They were moving. Nic was behind the wheel.

"No, dear. You've just had too much to drink," said Sarin, taking the cup from Trina's hand. "Come on, let's get you to bed. You can sleep it off and then go home." She took Trina's hand, leading her past Vee and into the bedroom.

Trina fell onto the black sheets. The room was spinning as she stared up at the ceiling.

Vee followed them in, standing on the side of the bed. She looked at Trina with a predatory glare.

"No, I'm sure we're moving," Trina said, sitting up.

Sarin pushed her back down, where she lay flat. Trina's leg hung off the edge of the bed, her feet not reaching the floor.

"Let's get you out of these," Sarin said, pulling at Trina's pants.

Trina wanted to fight, she did, but there was nothing left inside of her. Something had made her a zombie and she couldn't do much besides talk.

"No," Trina moaned, as her tight pants were pulled over her ass. Half of her wanted it, while the other half was terrified. Something was wrong, but she felt powerless. She knew she was drunk, but this was stronger.

She could feel herself getting wet as Sarin's nails dug into her hips. Trina's body betrayed her, giving in to the lust, which outweighed the fear. Sarin stared at her as she pulled the tight pants over her thighs.

Trina, in her fugue, wriggled out of her pants. Her eyes were closed and she was almost gasping for air. This was far from the lesbian experience with Jannet. This was something new, something different.

Sarin knelt on the floor in front of Trina's spread legs. She stared at her crotch, which was covered in a pair of black, cotton panties. She could smell her. The scent drove her wild. Gently, Sarin put her fingers in the waistband of Trina's panties.

Trina was in a trance. She was horny, more than she'd been in a while. The fear she'd once felt was gone. Her eyes were still closed, but she could feel Sarin in front of her. Something clicked in her head. Something that could ruin the entire night.

"Wait," Trina said, her eyes snapping open, looking down at the woman between her legs.

Sarin, who already started to work the underwear over Trina's wide hips, looked up at her.

"It's that time of the month," Trina said, embarrassed at her bodily functions. She looked down at Sarin.

Sarin kept tension on the underwear. Her gaze was on Trina's cleft, just hidden by the thin fabric.

Sarin looked up at her and smiled. "I know," she said, pulling the black panties off with a flourish.

Trina gasped, her sex free from the warm embrace of her undergarments. Her self-consciousness was out the window. She was horny. No, she was fucking horny and didn't care. She always considered herself straight, but at that moment she would've licked Sarin's pussy until the sun rose.

Sarin looked at the string hanging from Trina's vagina. It was tinted brown and hung low, nearly touching her anus. She wrapped her finger around the string, putting a little tension on it. Vee looked at her in anticipation, licking her lips.

Sarin pulled, just enough to get the tampon to move.

Trina moaned, eyes closed, basking in the pleasure. The coarseness of the tampon sliding out of her was almost erotic.

Sarin continued to pull until the bloody flower, a rose of red and white, coated in clots and gore, popped free. She brought it to her nose, breathing deep the scent of menstrual blood. She looked up at Vee, who was licking her lips at the treat in front of her.

Sarin tossed the bloody clump of cotton, which was quickly grabbed by Vee.

Vee, savoring the moment, dipped the bloody tampon in her mouth as if it were a teabag. She sucked, pulling every drop of blood she could from the cotton fibers.

Trina's heart was pounding. She opened her eyes, her embarrassment drifting away. Sarin's face was between her legs. The fear of her unsavory crotch was a distant memory.

Sarin kissed her thighs, both hands keeping her legs spread wide. She looked up at Vee, who'd finished sucking the last clots from the tampon.

Trina was coated in bliss. It felt like she was covered in warm honey. Her body was melting in pleasure; each breath Sarin breathed on her hungry cunt was nearly bringing her to orgasm. She looked down as Sarin looked up.

It was time.

Sarin changed in an instant. Her sweet smile, welcoming in every sense, was gone. Her mouth, once full of perfect, square teeth, now looked like a shark's mouth. Rows of razor-sharp bone lined an impossibly wide mouth. Sarin, her lust and hunger strangled by her self-control, now achieved the release it was looking for since the concert started. She bit into Trina's vagina, taking her labia off in one, bloody bite.

Trina took a deep breath, her lungs ready to unleash a horrid scream, but her mouth wouldn't open.

Vee's fingers, now tipped with claws, grabbed at the bottom of her chin, keeping her mouth shut. They dug into the soft flesh of her submental, just piercing her skin, as she pulled.

Trina's head was bent backward almost to the point of breaking. Her neck strained; muscles taught. Blood from Vee's nails ran down her jawline.

Vee smiled the way a wolf smiles at its prey. She snarled; her mouth sporting rows of hellacious teeth as she descended on

Trina's throat. Unholy teeth pierced flesh and Trina's dying breath entered Vee's mouth with a spray of blood.

Sarin left Trina's mangled vagina and made her way to pay dirt; the femoral artery. She bit the inside of Trina's thigh, almost to the bone. Warm blood shot into her mouth, nearly gagging her in its intensity. She drank greedily, watching Vee gorge herself from Trina's neck.

Finally, the flow stopped. Trina's corpse, which was pale in life, was the color of chalk. Her dark make-up was even starker in contrast. Her big eyes, once so full of life, gazed blankly at the ceiling of the trailer. A second mouth, this one jagged and weeping blood, smiled in death.

Vee and Sarin, full of sloshing blood, looked up from the mutilated corpse. They stared at each other, teeth crimson, but still hungry. No longer hungry for blood, but something else. Something more carnal, sexual.

The two vampires lunged at each other, hands pulling the other closer. Black lipstick and shark-like teeth mixed in a violent kiss. Tongues darted into salty mouths, feeling the sharpness of the other's teeth. Shirts were pulled off, nipples sucked.

Sarin stopped Vee, who was working at her pants. "I need him," she said, her pussy hungry for internal stimulation. Usually, Vee and Sarin would have no issues pleasing each other, but occasionally they'd bring Nic into their lovemaking. Something about the warmth of his human flesh inside of their cold bodies made them quiver.

Vee continued to work Sarin's pants off as the other vampire banged on the wall of the camper.

The camper began to drift to the right, slowing down until it came to a complete stop.

Nic emerged from the driver's seat. He knew what they needed and was happy to oblige them. Even though the mangled corpse of Trina was still on the bed, he was horny. This scene was one he was used to, even though it had taken him some time.

He, unlike the two vampires in front of him, didn't need blood to live. He was as human as they come, with human needs.

Sarin was nude. She was rubbing residual blood all over her body, her large and immortal breasts tinted red. She looked back at Nic, who was standing in the doorway. She pushed Vee on the bed and pulled her pants off.

Vee helped her, wiggling out of the bloody denim. She ripped her tank-top off, exposing her breasts. She kneaded her left nipple, pulling it hard. Her pussy needed attention and she was sure Sarin was in the giving mood. Gently, she put her right hand on the back of Sarin's head.

Sarin didn't need an invite to eat pussy, but she didn't mind. She smiled up at Vee, her teeth back to a more human-like form, and licked her lips.

Vee watched, her dead heart fluttering. The anticipation was almost too much.

Sarin let Vee guide her face to her bald slit. Her long tongue slithered out, entering the other vampire with a moan.

Sarin's own carnal needs ached. She needed to be filled. She raised her ass into the air, the only invite Nic should need.

Nic stared; Sarin's puckered anus and vagina were on display, calling his name.

Nic sprung his erection from his pants as he moved across the short room. Unceremoniously he slammed his cock into Sarin, her tightness taking him to the base.

With dead eyes, Trina watched it all.

2

ONE OF THEM

CAMERON SNYDER SAT at the empty table. He put his lunch tray down in front of him, setting his book bag on the seat next to him. He opened his bag pulling his well-worn copy of, *The Bighead* by Edward Lee out, and flipped it open. His stomach, growling at the anticipation of finally getting a meal, cramped. Cameron, careful not to get anything on his beloved book, began eating. The food was premade, canned, industrial slop, but there was a good chance it would be his only meal of the day.

Cameron stabbed at his tray, his plastic spork spearing canned green beans. He kept his eyes on his book as he brought the utensil to his mouth. A bean fell, bouncing off his light, reddish beard before landing on his *Slayer* t-shirt. He put the spork down and picked the bean up from its resting place. He popped it in his mouth and reopened his book.

"Jesus Christ, Snyder, did you just eat something off the floor?"

Cameron, again immersed in the perverted world Edward Lee had built in his novel, looked up. He stifled a groan, seeing three of the biggest assholes in the school standing in front of him.

Pat Dean, the one who'd asked him the question, was by far the biggest douche of them all.

"Are you fucking deaf?" Pat asked, taking a step closer to Cameron.

Cameron put his bookmark in the pages and closed the paperback. He didn't want to fight or argue with the trio of dick heads. He just wanted to eat his lunch in peace and read his book. That was all. He didn't fear them physically, even though Pat was fairly large. No, he feared them for their emotional assaults. The snide remarks, the phantom kicks in the hallway, his car being vandalized. If Pat Dean said you were a target, you were a target.

Cameron had been in Pat's crosshairs since 8th-grade football when he'd knocked him on his ass during a drill. Pat, who was and still is smaller than Cameron, couldn't live it down. He thought social status and money should influence your football abilities, not speed, size and talent. After that day the attacks began in earnest. Other boys, friends of Pat, targeted Cameron. They would make fun of his hand-me-down cleats, his mother's car, even his BO. He brushed it off and played hard, outplaying almost everyone else on the team. He was even making a push for starting running back, until his injury. Pat and another boy set up a well-timed chop block, breaking his leg. The break wasn't bad, but he missed the entire season. He and the coach knew that block was on purpose, but there was nothing they could do.

Now the boys were just starting their senior year and it seemed like Cameron couldn't escape the bully's attacks.

"No, Pat, I'm not deaf. Just trying to enjoy my lunch and catch up on some reading."

Tyler Brigs, a weaselly little shit, who always wore a flat

braided chain and too much cologne, grabbed the book from the table.

"What the fuck is this?" He asked, looking at the odd artwork of the cover. "*The Bighead*? Is this some kind of gay porn book? Are you a fucking fag, Snyder?"

Cameron, still trying to keep his cool, looked at the other boy. A few kids around them smelled the confrontation growing, hoping it would escalate into a full-on fistfight. That was the last thing Cameron needed was to get beat up and suspended.

"Can I just have my book back?" Cameron reached out. His other hand still held the spork, wet with green bean juice.

"This is almost as gay as your fucking t-shirt collection. What, did you get that shirt from one of mommy's boyfriends?" Pat said, louder now he had a growing audience. He smirked, garnering nods of approval from other kids around the table.

Cameron was fuming. He didn't speak, but his expression said it all. He wanted to stand up and punch Pat, break his perfect teeth, blacken his blue eyes and crack that nose. But, he couldn't. It wouldn't end well for him and he knew it. Rather, he said nothing, just stared at the other boys. This, more than anything, seemed to piss them off even more.

"Fuck this, I'm hungry," said Tyler, throwing the book at Cameron. The book slid across the table, hitting his bottle of iced tea. It teetered, rolling on the ridges along the bottom and tipped over. Peach tea spilled all over Cameron's lunch and book, some dripping onto his pants.

"What the fuck!" he said, jumping up to avoid any more mess. He grabbed his book, which luckily wasn't soaked.

"Oops, my bad," Tyler said. He could see the anger on the other boy's face and for a second thought they might have to fight.

"Here," the third boy, Alex, the silent one with who Cameron never really had too many problems, stepped forward. He held out $5. "Buy another lunch."

Cameron looked at the money. He wanted to take it, he deserved it, but his pride wouldn't let him. He couldn't let them know he needed the money; needed the food. He'd rather starve.

Pat grabbed the money and gave it back to Alex. "No, keep it," he looked back at Cameron, "he gets free lunches anyway. Don't cha?" He asked, damn well knowing he did. "Another fucking leech on the hardworking people of this town."

Alex took his money back, reluctantly putting it in his pocket. He didn't want to go against Pat. In an instant, he could be on his bad side and suddenly he'd be the one with the ruined lunch and target on his back.

"Come on, my food is getting cold," Tyler said, his torment of Cameron over for the time being.

The cafeteria, now that the excitement was over, resumed its normal dull roar.

Cameron wiped his book off and tossed the soggy napkin on his ruined lunch. He would've still eaten it; his stomach growling again, but he couldn't. He didn't dare eat the disgusting lunch in front of the rest of the kids.

He looked around, some people were still looking his way, making their private comments, laughing. Tyler, Alex, and Pat took their seats. The other kids at their table were laughing and giving out high-fives and fist bumps as if they'd accomplished a great task. Cameron put his head down and picked up his tray. He shouldered his bookbag and walked towards the garbage can.

Tara Springhauer nearly walked into him.

"Sorry," he said when she was clearly at fault. Cameron blushed at being so close to her. She was perfect in every way, at least in his eyes. Ever since second grade he had a crush on her. This youthful infatuation turned into teenage lust and would never stop. One of the main reasons was that she was nice. Not just nice to him, but nice to everyone. Of course, she was popular, but not a stuck-up bitch like so many of the others. No, she was genuinely nice and always had been. Over the years they'd been friendly, but far from friends. Cameron would talk to her here and there, but she tried to avoid him in public. She was nice, but not dumb. No one wanted to be seen with him, as if he had a scarlet letter on his chest. He didn't blame her, but it still hurt.

"It's ok," she said, about to toss her tray in the garbage. She looked back at Pat's table, the popular table. They were occupied with something on one of their cell phones. "Here," she said, handing him an apple wrapped in a napkin. "I don't have any cash, but I saved you this."

Cameron was stunned. He didn't even know what to say. Normally, Tara wouldn't talk with him in public, but she must've seen what happened. Maybe, just maybe this was the start of something. Probably not, but he could dream.

"Thanks," he said, taking the apple and tossing his tray. He barely finished before she walked away, leaving behind the scent of something exotic that left him tingling. Cameron adjusted his book bag and left the cafeteria. He took a big bite of the apple, the sweet juice running down his chin.

CAMERON DROVE his mom's old Ford Taurus. It was beaten to shit, but it ran just fine. That was in part, no wholly, because of him. Every dime he made went into the car and maintenance was always kept up. Well, almost always.

The radio was maxed out; the speakers (one of the few upgrades in the car) were throbbing with extreme metal band, *Pig Destroyer*. The music was fast, loud, and violent, exactly what he loved. The lyrics blended into a cacophony of ear-splitting sound that to the layman, sounded like noise. Not to Cameron, no it was art.

He banged on the steering wheel, trying to scream the lyrics with the lead singer, but it was no use. He didn't have the vocal cords or lungs for that. He always tried though, but usually ended up with a headache and sore throat.

After Tara had given him the apple his day had semi-improved. They had a substitute in English, which meant they were watching a shitty Shakespeare video. Cameron spent the whole period catching up on his reading, relishing the gore and depravity of the book. How he wished he could introduce the assholes from the cafeteria to the Bighead.

The apartment complex where he lived with his mother peeked out from behind a building. It wasn't much, but it was home. The tan brick and exposed air conditioner slots made it look cheap, which it was. That was the main reason they lived there.

Karen Snyder was far from mother of the year.

When Cameron was 10, his father was killed in a car accident. Since then, nothing has been the same. His mother was always a drinker, but his father would try to keep her in check. When he died nothing was stopping her from drowning in booze. Soon the life insurance money ran out, drank away, and vomited up. Then, they lost the house, the only house Cameron called home. Then the violence began.

Cameron knew his mother never loved him, even if she didn't say it. Oh, she played the role alright, but there was no love. She blamed him. She blamed him for ruining her body, which she claimed was supermodel status before pregnancy. Blamed him for forcing his father to work late to keep a roof over their heads. Blamed him for ruining her sleep on the nights when he was sick or had a bad dream. And above all, she blamed him for the death of his father.

The night Cameron's father was killed, Cam was running

around the house. He loved everything that was action and horror. He ran, pretending he was being chased by a slasher he called Mr. Blood n guts. His imagination, ever so vivid, brought him into the story a little too much. While was running, he tripped, smacking his forehead on the coffee table. His skin split in a burst of blood and he wailed. Karen, who was on her 4th scotch of the night, yelled at him for running and tried to stem the blood flow. It was no use. She called her husband, who'd taken the car to work. She told him what'd happened and that Cameron needed stitches, so he'd have to come home. He never made it. A drunk driver smashed him head-on, killing him instantly. Since that day his mother would barely look at him.

Shortly after the funeral things started going downhill. Karen was - more often than not -drunk and she was a nasty drunk. It started small, with a smack here and a smack there, but eventually, she twisted Cameron's arm so bad, it broke. That sobered her and after he lied for her and was cast up, she was nice. For a little while. Within days the beatings started back up again. The tiniest thing would set her off and then she'd erupt. Finally, when he was 13, Cameron had enough. His growth spurt hit him like an acne freight train and overnight he grew 8 inches and gained 60lbs. The thin, scared little boy was now in the body of a man. The next time his mother swung at him, he grabbed her arm. Unlike her, he didn't snap it, although he could feel how frail her bones were. She felt more avian than human. A look of fear and anger was embossed on her face, the scowl almost permanent.

Since then, she hadn't attempted to lay a hand on him. She used her slurred words to dig at him. Usually making fun of his weight, which wasn't bad at all, his acne scars, and even how he dressed. What a mother.

Cameron pulled into the complex. His good mood suddenly left him in a hurry. A beat-up truck was parked in his spot.

"What the fuck," he said, turning his music down. He drove

around the lot, to the back of the building and parked in a visitor's spot. He got out, locked the doors, and walked around to his apartment.

Every day the smell of the place would assault him, but within minutes, he'd get used to it. He walked into the apartment, keeping his shoes on. God only knew what was on the floor. The kitchen to his right was the main source of the sour smell. Dirty dishes, moldy pots, and rotten food were everywhere. He couldn't remember a time when his mother had cooked, let alone eaten anything from that cesspool. Every surface was slick with grease and filth. He knew there were roaches in there, he just didn't have the energy to try and get rid of them. The refrigerator hadn't been opened in days and when it was it smelled like death. Probably because Karen left a whole chicken in there for a month.

The carpet, which had once been a hideous shade of teal, was grey. It always felt damp and he could swear it would squelch underfoot.

The living room opened to the left. If anything was living in there it was mice and bugs. The couch was covered in takeout containers, empty beer and liquor bottles, and cigarette butts. The ashtrays had long since overflowed and Karen had taken to extinguishing her smokes on the arm of the couch. An old chair was next to the couch, but that was so covered in old clothes and past due bills it was not even visible.

Cameron heard voices from his mother's room. Someone was in there with her. The door opened.

"Hey, Cam," it was Ronnie, the super of the building. "What's up?" he asked, trying to discreetly adjust his wilting erection through his jeans. He blushed, not knowing the boy was there. "Good day at school?" he asked, stepping over a pizza box as he made his way to the door. "Oh, Karen," he said, turning back to talk to the disheveled woman on the threshold of the bedroom.

"Let me know if you have any other issues." He smiled and left the apartment.

Karen was a mess. Her hair was short, brown with wisps of grey, and looked like it hadn't been washed in months. It stuck up at every angle and if she didn't just have sex, she looked like it. Her shirt was stretched and hung off one shoulder. She didn't have on a bra and her breasts hung low and free. The button on her shorts was undone, and she pulled a pack of smokes from her back pocket.

"How was school?" she asked, slurring her words. She put a cigarette in her mouth and lit it.

"Fine," Cameron said, walking towards his room. He fished the keys out of his pocket. He hated doing it, but he had to lock the door to his bedroom or his mother would sell everything.

She leaned against the wall like she was holding it up. She hiccupped, burped, and coughed. Then, promptly put the cigarette in her mouth again.

Cameron put his hand on the door to his room and stopped. He was about to ask a question he didn't want to know the answer to.

"Mom, why was Ronnie here?" He stared at her.

Karen looked back, her glazed eyes locked on him, but not seeing. Her brain was firing on one cylinder and was straining to find a suitable reason. Anything but the truth.

The truth was unspoken but known. Karen Snyder, once a housewife and PTA member, was now a low-level prostitute. She wasn't a streetwalker and doubted she would stoop that low, but if a gentleman friend needed a little company, she was more than willing. Especially if they brought a bottle with them. A bottle of what, it didn't matter, but the stronger the better. Most of the guys who would come over made sure to fuck or get sucked off before giving her the booze. Once she was blackout drunk, she tended to get nasty or would puke and pass out.

"Nothing, just chatting," she said, holding back a bubble of hot vomit. She stifled it with the back of her hand and put her cigarette back in her mouth.

"Chatting?" he asked, nodding in annoyance. "I didn't know you used your cock for chatting."

"Hey, watch your fucking language," she slurred, pointing a dingy finger at him. "Ronnie is the super and came to check on something. That's it," she puffed away. The cigarette was down to the filter. She tossed it on the floor, extinguishing it with her flip flop. "And what the fuck do you care? Huh. As long as there's a roof over your fat, fucking head, what do you care!" She pulled another cigarette out, lighting it. "So, fucking what." The smoke bobbed up and down as she teared up. "So, fucking what if I suck a dick or get fucked. Huh? It keeps us here," she opened her arms as if displaying the apartment. "I do more for this fucking family than you ever have."

Cameron had enough. He tensed and was on the fringe of striking her. His mother, punching her in the face. That smug, fake crying, trying to elicit sympathy from him. No fucking way. He opened his door and walked into his room, his chamber of solitude. He slammed it in her face, turning the lock behind him.

CAMERON'S ROOM was the only clean room in the apartment. He wasn't a neat freak, but anything without mold growing on it was better than what was in the rest of the place. It wasn't much, but it was his. A twin bed was tucked in the corner, unmade, but the sheets were semi-clean. A small dresser was at the foot of the bed and piled with books. His outdated laptop was on a small folding table.

He tossed his book bag on his bed and grabbed his computer. He unplugged it and plopped onto his bed. Aimlessly, he scrolled through his various social media sites, but there was nothing besides useless drivel. He couldn't avoid it any longer and opened his internet browser.

Shaking and nervous, he began typing, *A Gift of Death* band into the search bar. He took a deep breath and hit enter.

The screen flashed and different pages began showing up. He scrolled through them taking in the pictures of the band. There weren't many and those he could find seemed distorted. They looked so cool on stage, Sarin, belting out their rough and violent lyrics. He loved their music and couldn't wait to see them again.

8 months prior, Cameron was scrolling through a social media page. He saw a contest for free concert tickets. He hadn't been to a show in ages and decided to throw his name in the hat, hoping he might score a ticket. The bands were obscure, but he didn't care, he just loved metal, and the louder the better. To his surprise, he won. The concert was nearly 2 hours away, but he was so excited to not have to spend another night in the shit-hole apartment, he didn't care about the drive.

The show was amazing, some of the best local bands he'd ever seen. And then, they came on.

The MC introduced them, but they didn't care. They took the stage with attitude and vigor and they were women. Sure, there are plenty of women in metal, but these two were something else. Cameron sat in a daze looking at them. He hardly noticed the male drummer tucked in the back. Their set was amazing, some of the best music he'd ever heard. He had to meet them and would stop at nothing to do so.

When the show ended, he wandered around, hoping they'd come back in for a drink. Most of the bands drank for free at a venue, so he was counting on it. When that didn't pan out, he began searching. He left the venue and walked around and then he saw it. A camper painted black with a red *AGOD* on the side of it. He knew that was it. As he approached, he stopped when he saw the drummer talking to another fan. The fan was young, maybe a little older than him, in his early 20s. He had on a short, black t-shirt and was already covered in tattoos.

Cameron watched from afar as the two men talked like old friends. He didn't care about the drummer, who he remembered was named Arsenic. No, he wanted to meet Sarin and Vee-exx. They talked and talked and finally both entered the camper. Without warning, the camper began moving.

Cameron was near his car and jumped in, watching the camper the whole time. Something was driving him. He needed to meet the band, to get an autograph, to be in their presence, something. He didn't have to wait long.

The camper pulled over on a wide shoulder and killed the lights.

Cameron did the same, only keeping his distance. Something was up and he knew it. He left his car running but turned the lights off. He crept along the shoulder like a thief in the night, until he was alongside the camper. It was rocking. He tried peeking in one window to get a glimpse of some wild sex, but they were blacked out. He moved around to the other side. A thin sliver of light crept out and he knew he hit pay dirt. Cameron put his eye to the chink in the blackness and nearly screamed.

The two women were biting the young man. Not only that, but they were eating pieces of him. Long, hellish tongues lapping up blood from the man, as he lay helpless under them. They didn't even look like women anymore. They looked like monsters. Their mouths were wide and full of shark-like teeth. Their fingers were tipped in black, razor-sharp claws. Even their eyes didn't look normal.

Cameron, having witnessed enough, ran back to his car. He spun tires as he pulled away, hoping he didn't see a black camper in his rearview. He drove straight through, on edge the entire time, until he reached his apartment. Never in his life had he been so happy to reach that shithole.

Days went by and he didn't tell anyone what he'd seen. No, they'd think he was crazy, well crazier than they already thought.

He kept thinking about it over and over and finally reality sunk in. They were vampires, or so he thought. Cameron, through the magic of the internet, searched for *A Gif of Death* at concerts. The only images were from night shows. Not only that but every image was distorted, like the camera was out of focus, at least on Vee and Sarin. Nic came in crystal clear.

Cameron thought about this, wondering what it was like. Would it be a good thing to be immortal, to feed on the living and live by night? Compared to the life he lived; death was a great alternative.

From that day forward, he'd been obsessed, hoping one day, they'd take him in as one of their own. He knew this was a long shot. In reality, he thought he might have hallucinated the whole thing. One thing was for certain, if they could take him away from his life, he'd go in an instant.

Cameron scrolled through the search findings until he found what he was looking for; a tour schedule. *A Gift of Death* was sporadic at best, usually just stopping at venues along their route, hoping to play a show. This time it was different. This time they'd booked a few places. Not only that, but they were heading his way. The venue was quite a distance, but that wouldn't stop him. He had a date and location.

Cameron sat back against his pillows, dreaming of his life away from this place.

His mother coughed in the next room. She kept coughing, harder and harder. Finally, she retched and a splash of vomit hit the floor.

He couldn't fucking wait to leave.

3

WHEN IN ROME

CYRIL VISSER WOKE to the sound of someone banging on his bedroom door. His eyes fluttered open, the pressure of a hangover assaulting his brain. His mouth tasted sour and vile, but there was a familiar taste lingering; semen.

Cyril realized he was nude, his bare chest exposed to the air, his crumpled sheets nestled around his crotch. He looked next to him and saw an all-too-common sight; a man he didn't know.

The man slept, his bare skin the color of a light coffee.

"Oh, fuck," Cyril said, rubbing his face. He looked at his nightstand and pushed aside a used condom to grab his phone. "At least my ass was protected," he said to himself as he checked the time.

The knocking came again. This time it sounded like a foot.

"Hey, wake the fuck up!" The person on the other side of the door yelled. "We're running late and need to get going."

"Ok," said Cyril, putting his phone down and rolling out of bed. He stood, stretched, and scratched his bare nuts. He looked over his shoulder when he heard the guy in bed moving around.

"Hey," the guy said.

Cyril looked at the young man and said a small prayer that he was of age.

"Morning," Cyril said, looking for his clothes. Well, looking for something decent to wear; his clothes were strewn about the room. He couldn't find underwear so he free-balled a pair of jeans. "It's closer to noon," he said, sitting down to put on a pair of mismatched socks. His head was pounding and all the movement wasn't doing him too well. He grabbed an open bottle of water and chugged it down. It was lukewarm and stale, but to him it was lifesaving. He stood up and put on a shirt, checking to see how bad it smelled before doing so. It was passable.

"So, last night was fun," the young man said, sitting up, the sheets around his lap. He smiled with a mouthful of perfect white teeth.

Cyril would have to take his word for it. He remembered very little. The aftertaste of cum and the used rubber were the only evidence he'd even had sex.

"Yeah, I'm sure it was," Cyril said, brushing his shoulder-length hair back. He grabbed a rubber band and put it in a tight ponytail. The sides of his head were buzzed low. His brother, Nestorious, told him it was a lesbian haircut, but Cyril didn't give a fuck. He needed to brush his teeth in the worst way and no time to deal with a clingy one-night stand. "Look, whatever your name is, I'm sure last night was an assfucking, cocksucking blast, but I need to get going, so…" He let the pause hang in the air.

The young man's face dropped. He was hoping for a little morning, or early noon action, but was being told to get the fuck out.

"Oh, I see how it is," he said, tossing the covers back. "I'll be on my way then," he grabbed his clothes and began to dress.

Another knock on the door, but this time the handle began turning.

"Cyril, let's fucking go," Nestor said, opening the door to his brother's room. It wasn't a shock to him to see a half-naked man, hastily dressing. Nestor looked at the man and back to his brother. "Is he even legal?" He pointed at the man with his thumb.

Cyril, who was rubbing crust from the corner of his eyes, shrugged. "I hope so," he said. "Hey, sweetie, how old are you?" He asked the embarrassed man.

"Fuck you," he said, pulling his shirt over his head and storming out.

"Have a good day," Cyril said after him.

"Are you fucking ready yet?" Nestor asked. He was dressed and ready and even had his coat on. "We got a lead on the Ryerson case and we need to get to the Have-a-rest motel in," he checked his watch, "15 minutes."

"Yeah, I'm good to go," Cyril said, pulling on a pair of loafers. "Just let me brush the cock taste out of my mouth and we can run." He smiled, knowing his brother didn't care for the gay talk.

"Jesus Christ, Cyril. That's disgusting." Nestor said, letting his brother walk by.

Cyril walked into the bathroom and turned on the sink. "So, tell me again what we're going to do?" he asked, putting toothpaste on his toothbrush.

Nestor stood in the doorway and pulled out his cell phone. "I think you need to cut back on the booze. It's destroying your brain." He said, clicking on an email. "Our client, Phillip Ryerson, you know, the guy who's paying us to do a job?"

Cyril looked in the mirror and flipped him off.

"Well, Mr. Ryerson thinks Mrs. Ryerson, Annette to be precise, is fucking someone else. He, our paying client, who expects stuff done on time, told us yesterday he believes his wife will be at the Have-a-rest motel," he checked the time, "in 10 minutes. So, if your teeth are thoroughly brushed, can we please get going?"

Cyril rinsed his mouth, checked his face for any crust, be his or someone else's, and turned. "All ready. Let's go catch a cheating whore."

———————

CYRIL AND NESTORIOUS VISSER, he never went by his full name, always Nestor, started their PI business shortly after high school. Both of them were taught by their father. Each of them had a knack for finding missing things and could root out a lie like no other. After their father's tragic death, the boys decided to found their agency. They floundered, like any budding business, but once word spread about their uncanny abilities, they were hired left and right. Until Nestor realized something.

He figured out it would be quite easy to blackmail these cheating spouses. Once they were confronted with the evidence against them, they had two options: money or sex. If they were men (he didn't share in his brother's homosexual tendencies) they could pay a handsome fee to get a clean report. And if they were women, well Nestor had other plans for them.

He enjoyed sex, but it was so bland sometimes. Usually, any girl he hooked up with it was the same thing; mild foreplay, boring positions, and a condom full of his spunk. He needed something more, something aggressive, but he was shy. Well not shy, but he didn't want anyone having leverage on him for some of his weird kinks. That was where the marks came in.

Before the case would begin, Nestor would decide if he was going to approach it legit or as a pervert. If he felt perverted, he'd do some research, finding some of the most off-center and vile fetishes people had. From there it was simple. He'd catch the adulterous slut and blackmail her. If she didn't take the proposal on his fetish, the proof would be given to the client. If she did, well things got fun. Mostly for him and rarely for her, but that was business.

Most people kept their mouths shut, but some didn't. Either they were physically injured, ill from his little experiments or so revolted they had to admit it. Word got around and business took a hit. It was a dark time for them and work was scarce, so Nestor decided to play it legit, until recently. He couldn't help it. There was something in him that urged his perversion and he couldn't explore it alone. Sure, there were others on the internet like him, but he wanted fetish virgins, not someone who was getting shit on the daily. Besides, he needed the blackmail to keep them quiet. He'd been lucky recently and no one had talked about his 'arrangements'. He was hoping to keep that going; the business couldn't take another hit.

Cyril had the passenger window down. He smoked a cigarette, letting the smoke trail behind him. He took a puff and looked at his brother.

Nestor had a wry grin on his face like he was thinking happy thoughts. "You're going perverted, aren't you?" Cyril asked.

Nestor was behind the wheel, a smile on his clean-shaven face. He looked over at his brother. "I didn't have a big lunch for nothing," he said, eyes back on the road.

"I don't even want to know," Cyril said, flicking his cigarette out of the window as they pulled into the parking lot of the motel.

"Just like he said," Nestor stated, parking in front of room 1-B. Three spots down was Annette's car. "Ok, wish me luck," he said, getting out of the car and walking into the main office.

The clerk, a middle-aged man who looked every bit a child molester, sat behind the counter. He was reading an issue of *Time* magazine, but a porno mag was clearly behind it. He looked greasy. Even his glasses seemed to have a film over them.

Nestor stood in front of the counter, flashing his best smile.

In reality, he wanted to reach over the desk, grab the pencil neck clerk and shake him until his fucking head popped off. No, he needed to play nice. He cleared his throat.

"Excuse me, sir," he said, trying to get the man's attention around the magazine.

The clerk looked up at the young man in front of him as if he didn't know he was there.

"Help you?" he mumbled, his attention going back to the magazine.

"Ah, yeah. I'm meeting a friend here and her phone must've died. Can you tell me what room Annette Ryerson is in?"

"Sorry," he said, not looking at him, "confidential. If she wants you," he looked at him and chuckled, "she'll find you."

Nestor's facade was cracking. He didn't want to come out of pocket for this, but he needed that info. He took a crumpled $10 bill from his pocket and slid it across the desk.

The clerk looked at it and back to him.

Nestor's youthful, kind face had changed. It now seemed angular and hard. Full of rage as his eye twitched ever so slightly.

"Look, I'm not asking to fuck your mother. I just want a room number. Take this," he pushed the bill further, almost knocking it on the floor, "as a token of my thanks." His grin widened to an almost maniacal look.

The clerk swiped the bill and closed his magazines. With a few clicks of a yellowish mouse, he had the information.

"She's in 1-E, but if you murder her, I'm going to the police." He opened the porno back up.

"Thank you, my good man," Nestor said, as he turned and walked out.

Cyril was sitting on the hood of the car, scrolling through some dating app and smoking another cigarette.

"Find her?" he asked.

"Yup, 1-E," Nestor said, walking past his brother to the room. He stopped outside of the door and had his ear up to it.

"Well?" asked Cyril.

"Shh," Nestor put a finger to his lips. He nodded. "Yup, they're fucking alright. Give me the snake."

Cyril pulled a long, fiber-optic camera from his pocket. It was coiled up tight. "Here," he said, handing it to Nestor.

Nestor checked to make sure a memory card was in the device and powered it on. He looked around and slid it under the door.

Cyril had his phone in hand and the Bluetooth app was already open. "Damn, you weren't kidding," he said, watching the couple having sex. "She's giving it her all."

Nestor looked over at his brother's phone.

Annette Reyerson, 38 years old, with two kids, and husband, was riding this mystery man so hard, it looked like she was going to break his cock off. Her tits bounced, nearly hitting her in the face, as she rode him.

Nestor was starting to get hard, but he'd have to wait. His turn was coming.

"I think that's enough," he said and pulled the snake back, coiling it up. He reached into his pocket and pulled his PI shield, which looked enough like a police shield. He cleared his throat and banged on the door. "Police," he said, loud enough for them to hear, but not loud enough for the other guests. He knocked again. "Police, open the door."

Rustling could be heard inside the room. Finally, the locks began to click.

"Yes, officer, can I help you?" The man said. The security chain was still fastened, only giving him a small portion to talk from. He wasn't much of a looker, but then again neither was Annette. He was sweating and red, his chubby body covered with a cheap robe.

"Sir, we need to speak with Mrs. Ryerson. May we come in?"

The man was flabbergasted. He didn't know what to say.

"Ah, there's no Mrs. Ryerson here. Just me," he said, not even believing his lie. It sounded forced, mainly because it was.

"Sir, please don't lie to me. I'd hate to have to bring you in on obstruction charges. Now, may we come in?"

He deflated and unfastened the chain. "I suppose," he said, opening the door.

The room stunk. First off it smelled dirty, like Cyril's room. The next smell was sex. Sweaty pussy and dirty balls made a foul, putrescent odor that seemed to float in the air. Nestor knew when he was done, the room was going to smell much worse.

The man nodded towards the closed bathroom door.

"Thank you," Nestor said, as he and Cyril walked towards the bathroom. "Mrs. Ryerson," he tapped his knuckles on the door. No answer. "Mrs. Ryerson, this is the police." He paused for dramatics.

Cyril looked at a rather wide dildo on the nightstand. He wrinkled his nose at the brown lump on the tip of it.

"It's about your husband," Nestor said.

"Her husband?" her lover gasped, in mock surprise. "I didn't know she was married," he feigned shock. He would never win an award for his acting, but the brothers didn't care. It was better if he left on his own. "I'm so upset," he said, pulling his pair of tighty-whities from his crumpled pants on the floor. He slid them on under his robe. His pants were next. "I've never been so insulted," he continued, dropping the robe to put his shirt on. "Absolutely unforgivable-" he continued his squawking as he walked out the room, slamming it for effect.

"Make sure he's gone and lock it," Nestor said to Cyril.

Cyril peeked out of the curtains and watched the man speed away. "Yeah, he's out." He locked the door.

"Annette, open up," Nestor said, tapping on the cheap wood. "Let's talk."

Slowly, the door cracked open. Annette stood with her robe wrapped tightly around her. Her brown hair was disheveled and her mascara was running.

"What the fuck do you want?" she squeaked, looking at both men.

Nestor looked harmless, with his close-cropped hair and clean shave. But it was his eyes that gave him away as anything but that.

"Phillip sent us," he said, watching the color drain out of her. "He knows, Annette." She started to speak, but he stopped her. "He knows something, but he doesn't know everything." He turned to Cyril. "Show her."

Cyril opened his cell phone and pulled up the video taken by the snake.

She was mortified, embarrassed, and scared. Exactly what Nestor wanted.

"Now, we can make this go away. I'll let you personally delete this from the phone and it can be over, but there's a price."

A look of hope and then desperation flashed over her face. "I can pay, but not a lot. Phil sees everything. He even found out about my private checking account. I might have a few hundred on me, but that's it."

Nestor shook his head. "No, no money. There's something else," he reached up and touched her robe.

Annette slapped his hand. "Get your fucking hands off me!" she yelled, color rising in her cheeks. "I'm not some fucking whore."

Nestor looked at the red mark on his hand. He wanted to use that hand to strangle her but kept his cool. He usually did, usually.

"Ok, that's fine." He spoke. "But we were hired to do a job and well, the job has to be completed. Best of luck." Then to Cyril. "She doesn't want to play ball, so let's go."

Cyril shrugged. "Good, I was a little worried about what fetish you picked this time." They walked to the door, unlocking it.

"Wait," Annette cried. "What do I have to do?" Tears ran down her face. When she first saw Nestor, she thought him handsome, now she was repulsed.

Nestor smiled at Cyril and turned around. "Nothing really. Just lay on the bed and I'll do the rest. Hell, I won't even make physical contact with you."

"That's it?" she asked, gripping the robe tighter. She wiped her nose with the sleeve. "Are you going to jerk off on me or something?"

"Ah, that's part of the surprise. I don't want to spoil the surprise," he said, a grin on his face. "Just lay down and close your eyes. It'll be over before you know it. Although, you may want to be nude for this. I've heard it can be messy."

Annette walked over to the bed and sat. "This will be over after this, right? You'll delete the video?"

"Cyril, give me your phone," Nestor said. He pulled up the video of her having sex with her lover. He showed her the screen and hit 'delete'. "See, in an act of good faith, I've already deleted it." He obviously forgot to mention the memory card, which he'd hang on to just in case. He handed the phone back to his brother. "Ok, now let's lose that robe and get started."

For a second, Annette thought about screaming and trying to run. She didn't know what the outcome would be, but she knew the cops would get called. That couldn't happen. She just needed to do what he wanted and be done with it. Hell, if she had to clean a shot of cum out of her hair, she would. As long as this ended and they went back and told Phil she wasn't cheating.

"Ok," she said, taking the robe off. Her body wasn't much to look at, but it wasn't bad. Her nipples were hard as rocks, centered on massive areolas that encompassed the entire lower portion of her breasts. She kept the robe around her crotch, but

Nestor had a good idea she wasn't well-groomed. Call it a hunch. She laid on the bed, her heart racing. Her head was on the end of it, her hair hanging off. "Like this?" She asked, looking up at him.

"Perfect," he said. "Now close your eyes and relax."

She did. Her heartbeat was visible through her ribcage.

Nestor looked at her face and smiled. He took two fingers and jammed them down the back of his throat.

Vomit, a torrent of partially digested food, water, and stomach acid, spewed from him. The orangish slurry, hot and thick, hit her full on in the mouth and nose.

Annette put her hands up, trying to stop the geyser of puke, but it was no use. Her eyes burned and she gagged when it entered her mouth. The smell, acidic and vile, pushed her over the edge. Her gorge rose as she sat up to avoid anymore. With a wet burp, she spewed her lunch, a tuna sub, all over the pillows.

Nestor was finished. He rinsed his mouth, cleared his sinuses, gagging one last time at the remaining vomit in there.

Cyril looked sick but held his stomach contents in.

Annette lay on the bed, crying hysterically, trying to clean her face of his and her vomit.

"Ready?" Nestor asked his brother, who was doing everything possible to not throw up.

"Yeah, that's a fucking understatement."

Nestor and Cyril left the room, going back to the car.

Nestor started the engine and popped a piece of gum in his mouth. He guided the car out of the parking lot and into traffic. "It's called Emetophilia," he said, keeping his eyes on the road. He blew a small bubble, snapping his gum. "It's a vomit fetish."

Cyril still looked ill. He lit a cigarette. "Clearly," he said, taking a long drag. He blew the smoke from his nose, hoping to purge the smell of vomit.

"Some even call it a 'Roman Shower'. Eh, it's not for me."

Nestor snapped his gum again. "Well, I can scratch it off the list."

"Thank fucking God for that," Cyril gagged a little.

"Let's go turn in this memory card and get paid," Nestor said, looking at his brother. "After that let's get something to eat. I'm starving and strangely craving a tuna sub."

4

FISH FOOD

Nic, Sarin, and Vee-Exx drove through the night. Before the deadly rays of sun crested the horizon, the trio drove into a state park. The park was mainly wetlands; a perfect place to dump the mangled corpse of Trina, their last meal.

For Sarin and Vee, it was simple. Their undead strength made moving the corpse next to nothing.

"How's this?" asked Nic, slowing down near a desolate stretch of wetlands.

"Fine," replied Sarin, who wasn't even looking. "Just pull over and we'll scatter her."

"Yeah, she'll be fish food by morning," Vee added.

Nic stopped and killed the headlights. He cranked the window down and lit up a cigarette. The night was alive. Bugs, bats, rodents...vampires. Everything was out and making noise. Granted the sound from the vampires was much different than that of the others. Their sound was that of flesh being ripped apart and flung deep into the marsh. It sounded like someone ripping fabric, not the corpse of a girl.

"Ok, we're all set," said Vee as they climbed back into the camper. Just like that, Trina was gone. Even if she were found, at least pieces of her, there would be no DNA. At least from Vee and Sarin. Nic never had any contact with the girl while she was in the camper, but if his DNA was found it was an easy fix. He could always say he met up with her after the show and they screwed around. It would tie him up for a while, but he'd be freed. Vee and Sarin would see to it one way or another.

Nic navigated his way through the swampland, keeping the camper on the tight roads. This would've been an ideal spot to sleep, but they didn't want to risk being so close to the corpse.

Cold arms wrapped around his neck. The apple scent coming off Sarin's skin was heavenly and slightly erotic.

"We're going to turn in," she said in his ear, her plump lips tickling his lobe. She nibbled him, just a taste, on his cheek.

Nic wanted to turn to her and kiss her, hoping it would turn into another bout of sex, but he couldn't. He needed to be disciplined and get them out of the park and away from the area.

"Yeah, once I find a spot, I'm going to park it and get some rest." He looked at her from the corner of his eye. "I just want to put some mileage between us and here. Just in case."

Sarin licked his face, smacking her lips. "That's why we love you, Nic. You're so smart and know what's best." She kissed him, leaving a smudge of black lipstick on his cheek. "I'll see you tonight." She said before walking back and opening the bedroom door. She and Vee double-checked the windows were blacked out and shut the door.

Nic drove, the dingy headlights of the camper cutting through the foggy gloom of the swamp. The suspension groaned and bounced with every rut and hole. He heard the vampires curse him from their blacked-out room.

———

5 YEARS PRIOR, if someone had told Roger Ecelstan his new name would be Arsenic and he'd be the drummer in a band full

of vampires, he would've had them committed. Well, 5 years later here he was. Roger was no more, he was now Nic.

It could've been worse; they could've eaten him as they planned on doing. Nic had been an avid music fan and was pretty damn good on the drums. He would go to any show he could, as long as it was some kind of rock. He would study them, mimic them, and above all admire them. One day he wanted to be on stage, with just his drums and sticks, banging away for a screaming crowd.

A new band, one he'd never heard of was in town at a small venue. He was off early and decided to check them out. That decision changed his life forever.

They were called *A Gift of Death* and they were made up of 2 females, one on vocals and bass, the other on guitar, and 1 guy, who was the drummer. He watched the show and loved it. Everything about it was metal to the core, from the outfits, to the names, lyrics and fast sounds. It was something he could get into. Throughout the performance, he could've sworn the lead singer- a busty, goth-looking woman named Sarin-was looking at him. He knew then he had to meet her. The other woman, Vee-Exx, was decent looking too and didn't wear a bra, but she was nothing compared to Sarin. The show ended with an ear-splitting guitar solo and a final growl from Sarin. He was in love.

He went out back after their set, hoping to meet the band. He certainly got his chance. Sarin was outside, standing in front of a black, camper. She had her cell phone in hand, pecking away at her screen. She didn't look startled when he walked up.

"Hello, I was just at the show and I have to say you guys fucking killed it. I play the drums and know a little about the bass, but let me tell you, that was one of the best sets I've seen in a while," he said, watching her slide her phone into her tight pants. He followed her hand as it patted the phone, which was tucked in the back pocket of her pants. As if underwater, he looked back up at her.

"I know," she said, smiling, the street lights reflecting off her teeth. "I noticed you in the crowd."

"You did?" he was swooning for the first time in his young life. He felt enamored, no, dazzled by this woman. It was like nothing he'd ever felt before.

"Do you want to come in?" She turned, gesturing to the door of the camper. "Have a drink with us?"

He couldn't resist if he wanted to and followed her, taking in the sight of her round ass.

Sarin poured him a drink. He didn't ask what it was, he didn't care. It was strong, but that was fine by him.

"So, where's the next show?" he asked, trying to make small talk. It was just him and Sarin, the other two members were nowhere to be seen.

"Oh, you know, here and there," she said, her free hand absently twirling her hair.

The driver's side door flew open and the drummer jumped behind the wheel.

"We have to go," he said, looking back at Sarin and the stranger at the table. "Who the fuck is he?" He waved it off. "I don't want to know." He started the engine and put it in gear, flying out of the lot.

"Excuse me a second," Sarin said, leaning up to the driver's seat.

"Who the fuck are you?" another voice said, this one coming from the now open bedroom door. Vee-Exx stood there with her green hair and free-hanging breasts. "Forget it, I don't care." She walked past him and up to the driver's seat with Sarin and the driver.

"What the fuck is going on?" Sarin asked. The camper narrowly avoided a parked car as it darted through the streets.

"I made a mistake," the drummer said. He was sweating and

constantly checking his mirrors. "I swear I'm done with it. This time I fucking mean it," he looked at his fellow bandmates.

The camper left the urban area and was cruising on a semi-rural town road.

"Did you rip off another fucking drug dealer?" Vee asked, her hands on her slender hips.

He didn't look, just kept driving and checking his mirrors.

"I asked you a quest-"

"Oh fuck," he said, stomping the gas. "They fucking found me." Headlights came racing up next to the struggling camper.

It was a large pick-up truck. It raced ahead of the camper and stomped the brakes.

"Fuck!" the driver yelled, practically standing on the brakes to avoid rear-ending the truck.

The doors on the truck opened and three rather intimidating individuals stepped out. Each was armed with a gun.

"I'll talk with them," the driver said, taking a deep breath. "I can smooth this over and we'll be on our way." He got out and approached the head of the small group. He didn't even get a word out before he was shot in the face. The back of his head split, his long hair dancing as a bullet exited his skull in a mist of gore. His corpse fell lifeless to the road, like a marionette with its strings cut. White skull and shredded brain peeked out from the wound. His face was distorted, the overpressure from the slug made his eyes bulge and weep blood.

Sarin and Vee looked at each other and then to the young man Sarin had brought back with her.

"Get the fuck out here," the man with the smoking pistol said. He was the epitome of bad news. He was tall, barrel-chested and covered in bad tattoos. His trucker-style hat said 'FUCK YOU' in bright red letters. The brown, cutoff flannel shirt was tight against his belly and the days' worth of growth on his cheeks was rough. "Get out here or we're turning this hunk of shit into Swiss fucking cheese." His other two men, each armed with submachine guns, aimed at the camper.

Sarin shrugged her shoulders and Vee smiled.

"Ok," Sarin said, "we're coming out." She climbed over the driver's seat, Vee following her. Both women stood by their fallen bandmate, his distorted face looking away from them. It was as if he knew what was to come.

"He had a debt and it needs to be paid," the man said, staring at the two women. "You two skanks are going to pay up for this asshole's problems."

Sarin put her hands down and crossed her arms under her breasts. "No, no I don't think that's going to happen."

"Yeah, shitbird, why don't you take your little fucking crew and get out of here before we lose our tempers," Vee said, her breasts jiggling with every animated word.

The three men laughed. They were 3 men against 2 women, plus they had guns.

"Listen, you creepy bitch, you and this skinny little slut are going to get the money this cocksucker owed," he pointed at the corpse with his gun, "or else."

Sarin took a step towards him. "Or else what?" she asked. Something changed in that instant. A power shift, an adjustment of fear, she couldn't put her finger on it, but it changed.

"Kill them," he said, bringing his gun to bear. The first round hit Sarin square in the chest...and did absolutely nothing.

She changed. This wasn't a perceived change; no this was purely physical. Her mouth sprouted rows of razor-sharp teeth and her fingers became hellish claws. She covered the distance in a flash and ripped the man's arm off, the gun still in his fist. Blood from his tattered brachial artery sprayed in her face. She licked the air a moment before she jumped onto his chest, like a cat. Her weight bore him to the ground, where she took his throat out in one vicious bite. He didn't even get a chance to scream. She drank greedily but was disturbed when more bullets hit her.

Vee had eviscerated the closest gunman to her, his shredded intestines leaking shit and blood. Bullets stung her but did little to slow her down.

Guns didn't scare the vampires - unless it was a bullet anointed with holy water and blessed by a pure priest - then they'd worry, but these were just run-of-the-mill, lead, and copper bullets.

Vee and Sarin circled the last gunman, who tried to run when he realized he was out of ammo. He didn't get far.

Vee jumped on his back, leaping from where she stood. She dug rents in his flesh, seeking his soft eyes. She found them, ripping through the lids and popping them like grapes.

Sarin was in full bloodlust and wanted in on the kill. She came in low, biting the back of his left knee out. Tendons poked out of his mangled flesh as he fell to the ground. They ripped into him; hungry mouths craved his full arteries. Long, sharp teeth sunk deep, releasing blood from its prison and into their waiting mouths.

Their guest, the young man, and fan who Sarin brought aboard, watched the whole thing. He'd long since pissed his pants and he was wondering what his next course of action was going to be.

The two vampires, their faces slick with crimson, walked back over to the camper and got back in. They stopped, forgetting he was there. They changed back, looking like humans again, albeit still covered in sticky blood.

"What are we going to do with him?" Vee asked, looking at the scared man covered in his urine.

Sarin smiled. "You said you played the drums, didn't you?"

He was petrified but thought he was nodding.

"Great, you're hired." She walked past him and grabbed a roll of paper towels. She wiped her face and handed the roll to Vee. "Get in the driver's seat and fucking drive."

He did and never looked back.

IT HAD BEEN over two hours since they dumped the body of the vampires' last meal. Nic was nodding off at the wheel and decided it was time for a little shut-eye. He coasted the camper onto a wide pull-off and killed the engine. He opened his phone and pulled up his email. Quickly, he sent a confirmation about their upcoming show. He silenced his phone and climbed into his small loft bunk above the front seats. Within minutes he was asleep. He didn't dream and for that, he was grateful.

5

PAY DAY

NESTOR AWOKE the next morning a couple of thousand dollars richer and felt great.

Phillip, his last client, was angry, but a little relieved to have video evidence of his wife, Annette, cheating on him.

Nestor figured it was because Phillip was also cheating and planning on getting a divorce. That video of Annette riding the cock of her mystery lover was more than enough to grant him a divorce with little to no alimony. Nestor left out the part of vomiting on the woman. If she wanted to tell her future ex-husband about that, then let her.

Nestor celebrated by watching some disgusting scat porn, which didn't pique his interest, but was more than enough to arouse him. A couple of shots of whiskey and a handful of lube was all he needed. He slept like a drunken baby.

Cyril, on the other hand, liked to celebrate with warm flesh. Within minutes of getting paid, he was on his way to meet the hook-up he found on one of the many dating apps he used. This time he came home alone and was sleeping off the night of cocaine, sex, and alcohol.

Nestor awoke, the sunlight burning his hungover eyes. A shrill sound was blaring and tore through his skull.

"What the fuck?" he moaned, looking for the source of his torment. His phone was ringing on the nightstand. He reached for it without lifting his head. His hand pushed a soggy, crumpled tissue onto the floor as he grabbed the phone. It was an unknown number, which wasn't uncommon. He didn't have many friends and those he did have wouldn't call; they'd text. He did his best to focus his eyes and pressed the green button.

"Hello," he mumbled into the phone. Nestor sat up in bed and rubbed his face.

"Ah, yes, I'm looking for the Visser Brothers Agency." The man on the other line said.

Nestor did his best to wake himself up, especially if this was going to be a business call.

"Yes, this is Nestor Visser. How can I help you?" He tried sounding not exhausted and hungover and hoped it worked.

"I would like to hire you and your brother, of course, for some delicate work."

Nestor knew he had a full day of binge-watching TV and eating take-out. It was always his ritual after a job well done. He didn't feel like taking on another job right away, especially since his account was fat.

"Ah, now isn't the best time, Mr…"

"Oh, I'm sorry. My name is John Calderon. My son, Nathan, is missing." He paused.

Nestor could hear the man sniffling like he was sucking up snot from crying. He looked up at the ceiling, willing the call to be over so he could start his day.

"I'm sorry for that," John said, composing himself. "As I was saying, my son has gone missing and I was told you two were the ones I needed to contact."

Nestor could only imagine who'd recommended them. Sure,

they were good at their jobs, but they didn't do missing persons. They did PI shit, like catching cheaters and such.

"Sir, I'm sorry, but we really don't work on missing persons. That's more a police matter. I'd be happy to refer you to —,"

"No," John snapped. "It has to be you two. You're the only ones who can take this job and put this to rest."

Nestor took a deep breath, calming his nerves. He wanted to reach through the phone and strangle the man on the other end.

"Look, bud, I know you're upset, but I can't help you. Now, if you'd like, I can give you the direct line to missing persons at the police department. They'd be happy to assist you." Nestor finished, he was shocked, thinking he was going to be cut off again.

"I need you and your brother. This isn't just a missing person; this needs your skills." He paused, as if collecting himself. "I know what work you did with your father."

Nestor inhaled, goosebumps covering his bare chest.

"It can only be you two," John said, leaving it at that.

Nestor sat dumbfounded in silence. He thought he was having a nightmare, a terrifying blast from his past. No, he knew this was real. He shuddered.

"Meet me at the old mini-mall lot in an hour. I'll be around back." He hung up, leaving nothing but dead air in Nestor's ear.

———

CYRIL SAT in the passenger seat. He wore a dark pair of sunglasses and was nursing a cigarette and a bottle of water. His long hair was messy, so he put on his rarely used baseball hat.

"Are we going to take this job?" He asked Nestor, not bothering to look at his brother.

"I don't know," Nestor said, his eyes locked on the road. "I don't know," he bit at a weeping cuticle, spitting the bit of nail and flesh on the floor. "I know what dad would want us to do."

Cyril took a drag of his cigarette and blew the smoke from his nose. He licked his dry lips and said, "I know, I know."

"Let's hear him out before we make any decisions," Nestor said, hitting his blinker to turn into the closed mini-mall parking lot. He circled around the building, his tires popping old beer bottles and flattening cigarette butts.

Cyril threw his cigarette out the window, adding to the mess. "There he is," he said.

A man, who looked to be in his early 50s, sat leaning on the hood of a Range Rover. He had a hand-rolled cigarette to his lips and he puffed deeply.

Nestor pulled up near the car. "Ready?" He asked Cyril, who was sniffing the air.

"He's smoking a joint," he laughed. "Huh, the old guy might be alright after all."

John dropped the joint onto the cracked pavement and put it out with boots that cost more than Nestor and Cyril's car. "Gentlemen," he said, shaking each of their hands.

Nestor looked at him. He was a good judge of character, a reason he hated mirrors.

John looked about as ordinary as they come; average height, receding hairline with a flattering haircut, a small gut pressing against a designer t-shirt. He screamed upper middle class if not low upper class, and his handshake was wet and limp.

Nestor discretely wiped his palm on his jeans. Even after masturbating to shit porn, the man's handshake still made him feel gross.

"Thank you both for coming," John said after shaking Cyril's hand.

The younger Visser brother wiped his hand as well, looking slightly repulsed. That was a lot for Cyril considering he ate strange assholes on a near nightly basis.

"No problem," said Nestor, getting right to business. "Our

time is valuable, so please do share why you called us almost an hour from our home."

John licked his lips and opened the driver's side door on the Range Rover. He pulled out a manilla folder and handed it to Nestor.

"Here. This is everything I have on them."

Nestor flipped through the documents; pics of a metal band, creeper pictures of them at night, but only the male member during the day, a black camper with '*AGOD*' in red letters on the side.

"Them? I thought we were looking for your son, not multiple people?" Cyril asked, looking over at the folder with his brother.

"Well, I may have told a little white lie to get you here." He took an old-school, metal cigarette case from his pocket. He opened it and pulled out another joint. "I know where my son is," he said, lighting the pungent weed.

"Oh," Nestor said, looking up from the file. "And where might that be?"

John flicked his lighter closed with a flourish. "Dead. Dead and fucking buried. That's where." He pointed at a picture of what appeared to be two women. Their faces were blurred. Their faces were blurred in every picture. The only one who was clear was the drummer, the only male in the trio. "These fucking cunts killed him."

Nestor flipped through the file, looking at scanned copies of newspaper clippings. Black and white pictures of mangled bodies, some in various stages of decay. He'd seen enough and closed the file. He looked up at John, who was puffing on his joint.

"And I want you two to kill them. All of them," he said, looking both of them square in the eyes.

"Wait a minute," Cyril said, "I don't know what you heard, but we're not hitmen." He tapped his brother on the arm. "Come on, let's go. This guy is fucking nuts." He started walking away, hoping Nestor would follow.

"Sorry about your son, but this isn't our line of work." He handed the file back. "Sorry," Nestor turned and began walking.

"Oh no, this is you, this has always been you and your family," John said, flicking his joint away and walking up to them in a lingering cloud of weed smoke. "The Visser name is a good name, a name of vengeance and justice." He was close now, close enough they could smell not only weed but alcohol on his breath. "I knew your father. I know one of these," he held up the file, "beasts, killed him. No boys, this is all you. From your family's days in the old country, until now, vampires trembled when a Visser was on their trail."

Nestor and Cyril looked at each other. The night their father was killed was their last night hunting monsters. It was easier, safer, and more fun extorting adulterers. Besides, they've never hunted without their father.

Nestor broke eye contact with his brother, who had a submissive look on his face, and turned to John.

"If we do this, it won't be cheap."

"Name your price." He smiled. His gums were receding and his teeth looked like they were barely hanging on.

With all that money, he should've fixed that fucked up smile, Nestor thought.

"One hundred thousand," he peeked at Cyril out of the corner of his eye. "Each."

John's smile widened even more. "Let's make it two hundred each, shall we."

Cyril and Nestor nearly fainted. That was life-changing money. They could get an office, updated equipment, hell maybe even hire a secretary. If they survived. They weren't after slutty wives or asshole husbands; no, they were hunting immortal killing machines that likely had been around for hundreds of years.

John pulled a checkbook from his back pocket. He scrawled on the first one, ripped it and handed it to Nestor and did the same with the next, handing it to Cyril.

"There, half upfront." He scrawled out another one. "And here's an extra ten thousand for expenses along the way."

Nestor looked at the checks in his hand like they were a mirage, afraid to look away in fear they would vanish.

"I've even made it easier for you," John flipped through the folder and held up a concert flier. It was shitty cut and paste, but the art wasn't important, what was on it was. "It seems our little trio will be passing close by in two days." He put the picture back in the folder and slapped it against Nestor's chest. "I want them all fucking dead."

Nestor looked at Cyril, who was folding up his check and putting it in his wallet. They locked eyes and nodded.

"John, my good man, you have a deal," Nestor shook his limp, wet hand. Cyril followed suit.

"Excellent. I look forward to hearing from you. Please make them suffer if you can." John turned and opened the door to the SUV. It started with a throaty growl and sped off.

"Fuck," Cyril said, taking his hat off and running his fingers through his hair. "What the fuck did we get ourselves into?" He kicked a crushed soda can watching it pinwheel across the blacktop. "Can we even do this without dad?"

Nestor stared. Not at anything in particular, just gazing into the distance. His eyes were aware of the graffiti and shattered windows of the old mini-mall, but they didn't truly see. No, they were playing the death of their father over and over.

The vampire, a small girl, looked so much like Lucy. Their father cried seeing her, thinking his dead daughter had come back. He'd been warned about her, told it was a young-looking vampire, but his heart broke seeing her. With one bite she tore his throat out. Cyril and Nestor, just barely old enough to drive, shot the creature with sacred bullets, sapping her strength before they were able to burn her. That had been their last hunt.

Nestor wiped a thin mist of tears from his eyes and looked at his brother.

"Yeah, we can do it." He put his hand on Cyril's shoulder, squeezing. "Let's go home and see if we can find his stuff."

"Ok," Cyril said, wiping his tears, "but first let's stop at the bank."

Nestor laughed and pulled his brother in for a one-arm hug. "Great idea."

6

NICKEL-PLATED DEATH

CAMERON SAT ON HIS BED, his laptop in front of him. He was scrolling through his mindless social media.

It was Friday night and he was home. His mother was in her room - the TV turned up to max - as if that would block the sounds of her getting fucked by God only knew who.

Cameron's day in school had been like almost every other one; shitty classes filled with him sneak-reading a book (he'd just started Dustin LaValley's *Spinner*), followed by lunch, which went well, more shitty classes, and finally, the drive home.

When he got home, there was surprisingly something to eat. Whatever guy his mother had in her room had been kind enough to bring a pizza. Cameron helped himself to half of it, eating in his room.

He scrolled, but wasn't paying attention. The concert was Saturday, just over 24 hours away. His stomach fluttered thinking of what that meant. Tomorrow night, he was going to die. One way or another. He was sick of living and if he couldn't be undead, he would settle for just dead.

His phone dinged with a text message. He had a few buddies, but when he looked down, he realized it wasn't a saved number.

"Hey, this is Tara," he read the first line to himself. He sat up, his eyes scanning the message. "I'm sorry about what those assholes did to you the other day. I'm happy I was able to save you the apple." He read it over and over, out loud to himself. This was the perfect way to cap off the shit week.

His fingers flew over the screen, speaking as he wrote, "Hey. Yeah, no worries. It was all good. Thnx for the apple. It was great." He read it over and hit send.

"LOL, an apple a day," he read her message, his teenage heart fluttering. Another message popped up, this one on Snip-chat, a video and picture sharing app. Snip-chat was great because whatever you sent disappeared seconds later, unlike text, which lasts forever.

He clicked on it and saw a picture of Tara at a party. She looked amazing, but then again, she always did. He could see the usual douche-nozzles in the background, but he didn't care. She was messaging him.

"This party is lame," she wrote in the caption of her picture.

Cameron didn't think it was lame. He wished he was there with her. His mother's bed sounded like it was going to break or come through the wall.

"LOL, doesn't look 2 bad," he replied.

Her text bubble showed she was writing. "Eh, it's ok." Her text bubble lit up again, showing there was more to come. "Hey, can I make it up to you? You know, for what they did the other day?" Cameron read the text.

"No, it's ok. No worries," he wrote.

A new picture message popped up on Snip-chat. His finger hovered over it. He pressed it, his heart racing.

It was her in a bathroom, with her shirt pulled up. Her perky, milky-white C cups stared back at him. Tight nipples sat centered in light pink areolas.

Cameron's cock was immediately hard. So hard, he didn't

think it had ever been that hard in his life. He unzipped his pants, letting it free from the denim prison.

"See anything you like?" She wrote back, the picture disappearing.

"Ah, fuck yeah," he said to himself, thinking of a message that didn't sound too creepy. "Well, that was certainly a pleasant surprise," he wrote, his left hand absently stroking his dick.

Her text bubble popped up.

Cameron knew what she was going to ask for and he was ready. Never in his life had he sent a dick pic, but for her, he would. Besides, on Snip-chat the pictures delete themselves.

"Ok, well you saw me, now let me see you?" There it was. The message he'd expected. He stood up and grabbed his desk lamp. Lighting was a very important thing.

———

"Do you think he bought it?" Pat asked, looking at Tara's phone.

"Come on, man. My cut and paste skills are on point. Besides, the lighting in the bathroom was perfect for it. Lighting is everything." Tyler said.

Tara had to admit, the pair of tits they'd found on the internet were pretty close to what hers looked like. It was uncanny, considering Tyler had never seen them. She hoped Cameron didn't fall for it, she truly did. She was up for a joke here and there, but he didn't deserve this. At the end of the day, she was popular enough to stop this, to call it quits. It was her phone and she didn't need a bunch of immature, drunk assholes grabbing at it. She could've stopped it, but she didn't. An alert for a new picture message popped up.

"Oh, shit. He sent it." Pat yelled, the crowd gathering around him. Everyone had their cell phones out, ready to take a picture of the screen. "Hit it," he said to Tara.

She had butterflies. The crowd was cheering and looking on, waiting on her. She hit the button.

The crowd yelled and cheered, some laughing. It was a dick pic alright, but taken in the most unflattering of ways.

Cameron had held his cell phone under his crotch, getting his hairy balls and asshole in the picture. Not only that but his face was clear as day. Apparently, no one told him to never show your face in a nude pic.

Pat ripped the phone from Tara's hands.

"Hey, dick, give it back."

"In a minute," he said, screenshotting the image. He quickly sent it to his phone, which vibrated in his pocket. He gave her the phone back and opened his. "Oh my God, look at his gross ass," he laughed, showing everyone around him.

"Blech," Marley, another popular socialite, who had a growing pill problem, said. "I think I can smell the crotch cheese from here." She put a hand over her nose. "Get it away," she waved her hand at the phone.

Pat laughed.

Then, he opened his social media.

CAMERON KNEW it was a bad idea the second he hit 'send'. It was too late; the message left his phone and was on its way to Tara. He didn't know what to expect and had never taken a dick pic before. He hoped it was flattering, maybe enough for her to send more or maybe actually talk to him.

His phone flashed and the message, 'your image has been screenshotted' popped up. His stomach dropped like he was on a rollercoaster. It was his father's death all over again, but this felt worse. He knew it then and there; his life was over. Cameron closed the app and opened his laptop. He jumped on his social media sites and nearly fainted.

His cock, hairy balls, and ass were everywhere, shared by Patrick Dean. He knew the images would get taken down, but that wasn't the point. Everyone in the student body would see the pictures. The damage was done.

Cameron slammed the laptop shut and pushed it off his lap. He cried, hard. Harder than he had in years. All the torment, the teasing, the hungry nights followed by abusive mornings. The strange men and filth of the apartment, all crashed down on him.

He slid off the bed onto the floor. He rooted around under his bed, dust clinging to his tears and snot. Boxes and bags flew out, thrown haphazardly around the room until he found it.

The grey, metal box was cool in his hands. The keyhole stared up at him, begging to be unlocked.

Cameron put the box on his bed and found the key he'd hidden under the molding of the window sill. He opened the box and looked inside.

Nickel-plated death looked back. When his father was alive, he always kept his Colt 1911, .45ACP caliber handgun locked away. He knew Cameron was a curious boy and didn't want to have a tragedy on his hands.

After his father had died, Cameron stole the gun. His mother was too drunk and upset to even notice it was gone. If she had found it, it would've been sold years ago to keep her in booze.

Cameron picked it up, electricity flowing through the steel. It smelled of gun oil, a scent that would always remind him of his father. He pulled back the slide, checking the chamber. It was empty as he knew it would be, but you were always supposed to check. He grabbed a magazine full of ammo. Each bullet was a squat, fat thing, with a hollow point in the front. The gleaming brass casings reflected his tear-streaked face. He slammed the magazine into the gun and pulled the slide, chambering a round. For a second, he thought about putting it to his temple and blowing his fucking brains out. Would he feel the hollow point enter his skull? Would it hurt as it filled with his bone and brain, as it passed through? He stared at it as if looking into the void. No, he'd rather fucking kill with it than die by it. It would be easy to bring to school. Keep it under his shirt and in class pull it out and start blasting. Starting with Pat first and working his way down the hierarchy of assholes.

The vampires. That was his goal. He took a deep breath, his hand tight on the grip, and began to relax. With practiced hands, he de-cocked the pistol and brought the hammer forward. His father told him never to carry a gun with the hammer back, especially without a holster. Cameron made sure the safety was on and tucked it into his belt. He felt like a gangster. He took another magazine from the box. It too was loaded with hollow points and stuffed it into his pants pocket. This was it; he knew it.

Cameron threw a duffle bag on his bed and started packing. He filled it with clothes, his few toiletries and of course, a couple of books. He put on a black hoodie, this one with an unreadable band's name on the front of it. He took one last look at his room, knowing without a doubt he'd never be back.

Cameron left, the sounds of violent sex still pouring from his mother's room. He took the rest of the pizza on the way out of the apartment.

7

BONE SAW

HELEN O'SHEA, Irish immigrant, daughter to Liam and Saoirse O'Shea, held a wounded Union soldier down as the doctor sawed off his leg.

The man screamed and bucked as the dull saw blade cut through bone. The laudanum was weak and wasn't doing much to stem the man's agony. Blood sprayed as the saw hissed against the exposed femur.

"For fuck's sake, we need more men in here!" The doctor shouted, not being able to keep the leg still enough for the saw to do the work.

Helen did all she could, but her petite frame was no use for the man on the table.

This scene was played out around her. Death, dismemberment and infection stunk up the air in the canvas medical tent.

The battle, a big one by her standards, had ended almost an hour ago, but wounded men were still pouring in. Many were too far gone for help and just given a large shot of opium to help usher them into death's sweet embrace. The man she was holding back had taken a cannonball to the knee, mangling his leg. It was a lost cause and was evident it needed immediate amputation.

"Nurse," the doctor said to Helen. He was old, too old to be on a battlefield. He should be in a small-town practicing medicine, not in the hills of Pennsylvania amputating a man's leg. "We need to keep him still or this leg is never going to come off." He looked crazy; his uniform spattered with blood in every stage of drying.

Helen nodded and put as much weight as she could, trying to keep him down on the table.

The bone saw began its rhythmic dance, biting deep into the whiteness of the femur.

When Helen first saw an amputation, she puked. Now, fourteen battles into her nursing career, she didn't care. The blood and screams were now almost background noise to her. She didn't know if it was a blessing or a curse.

The wounded soldier went still and quiet. Helen put her ear to his chest and looked at the doctor.

"He's passed out," she said, thanking the Lord for that. She didn't know how much longer she was going to be able to hold him down.

"Ok, let's get this leg off and him stitched up." The doctor cut, sweat beading on his wrinkled brow. The lower half of the man's leg fell off, hitting the bloody soil with a thump. "Use the fish mouth and sew him up." The doctor said to her, wiping his bloody hands and saw on a towel attached to his belt.

Helen grabbed a needle and gut, examining the stump of the leg. The fish mouth method was when the surgeon would use flaps of the patient's skin and sew it over, creating a smooth stump. Helen was excellent at sewing and set to the man's wounds immediately.

More men piled in, screaming as they were tossed onto gore-streaked tables. Helen finished her task and moved onto another patient.

"No," the doctor said as she walked over. He was sawing a foot off, but stopped mid stroke to look at her. "Doctor St. Claire needs nurses in the North medical tent."

Helen looked at him, taking in what he was saying. She didn't know why she had to leave this tent. The men in there were overwhelmed, yet they were sending her away.

"Ok," she nodded, walking towards the exit of the medical tent. She stopped to dip her hands in bloody water on the way out. It was as clean as they'd get for the next few hours. She dried them on her already gory smock.

The camp was organized chaos. Men, who weren't injured, sat around fires eating chunks of salt pork and hardtack. They laughed and smoked tobacco, joking as if their friends weren't bleeding to death feet away in a tent. Litters carried by horses, men in wagons, streamed by, each full of corpses or soon-to-be corpses.

Helen had to be careful to avoid getting run over, less she'd become another cold body. Not that anyone would care about the Irish girl who was run down by a horse.

She moved through the camp, which was only set up a few days prior. Quickly, she lost her bearings, peeking in every large tent she could find. The lanterns were few and far between, but the moon was full. She was on the fringes of the camp and beyond it was only the woods. Sentries should have long ago stopped her, but none were seen. She kept walking, leaving the commotion of the camp behind her. The quiet slid over her like warm clothes, rich and inviting. She needed the reprieve, if only for a few minutes of silence. Hopefully, the sentries didn't decide to come back to their posts and shoot her when she returned.

She was in a field, the small patch between the camp and wood line, and far enough to not hear anything besides crickets and other creatures of the night. She did hear something else; a stream. The thought of actually cleaning herself under running water was a siren's call. She didn't have soap, but just to feel her skin in the cool, cleansing waters would be enough. Besides, the night was hot and the next day would only be hotter.

Helen used the light of the full moon and walked into the tree line. She followed the sound of water and didn't have to go far. The silvery moon reflected off the small creek. It didn't look too deep, but appeared cool and inviting.

Helen peeled her tacky, bloody clothes off. The night air kissed her flesh, making goosebumps. Her nipples went rigid as her feet entered the water. She kept her footing as she waded forward, the cold water snatching her breath away. In Ireland, she would always play in the brook behind her parent's farm. She spent many hours in the water and her footing was always sure. Helen gasped as the water reached her thatch of black pubic hair. She took a calming breath, realizing she'd reached the deepest point of the water and submerged herself.

The dark inkiness of the water was like a tomb. The gentle throb of the current pulled her, ever so gently, willing her to come away from there. Away from death, dismemberment and blood. When she emerged, she wished she'd taken the water up on its offer.

Two men stood on the bank of the creek, near her crumpled and bloody clothes. Helen dipped down, covering her breasts under the water.

"Oh, pardon me, ma'am," a soldier wearing an open jacket said. He had a long mustache, common amongst the soldiers. His face was young, but there was something off about him. If Helen had to put a word on it, it was sour. There was something sour about that man.

The one next to him barely looked old enough to shave and thanks to the loose laws and need for men, he probably was.

"You seem to be lost," Helen said, mustering up some nerves. Inside she was terrified. She knew what could happen to a woman on the battlefield. Sometimes death wasn't the worst thing.

"Nope," the man said, pulling a long knife from his belt. He began picking at his nails with it. He looked back at her, sucking a drop of blood from his thumb. "Nope, we're in the right spot." He smiled with rotten teeth. The other man was silent, just looking as if she were the first naked woman he'd ever seen. "I was looking for the nurse with big titties who could help me." He reached into his pants and pulled out a large, erect cock. "See, I got this issue," he said, pointing at her with his penis. "I can't seem to make this hardon go away. I was hoping you might be able to help me there." He grinned a lupin grin.

Helen knew she was in trouble. She did not doubt that, but the question was how was she going to get out of it. Under the water, her hand felt for a suitable rock. She had nothing else and the two men were bigger than her and appeared drunk. She grabbed one, holding it tight as if it were a talisman to ward them off. It didn't work.

"Now, if you don't come on out and help me with this," he looked at his dick in his hand, "big problem, I'm gonna have to send Otis in to fetch ya."

The other man, Otis, looked at him and said, "Why do I have to go in the water?"

He looked at Otis and said, "Because I'm your goddamn superior and if you don't want to swing for desertion, you'll do as I say." He looked back at Helen, who was contemplating running back towards camp screaming. She'd be in her birthday suit and might get shot by the sentries, but that was better than being raped and murdered. "Now, get up here and take care of this pecker, or we're gonna fish ya out."

Helen didn't move, just squeezed the rock tight, waiting for them to make their move.

"Otis, go'en fetch her up."

Otis looked at the man and sighed. He had no choice as he stepped into the chilly water.

Helen waited, knowing she might only get one shot.

Otis waded in closer and reached for her.

With every ounce of strength possible, she swung. And hit his arm. The rock bounced from her grip, splashing in the water.

"Owe, you fucking hit me," Otis said, his hand rubbing his bruised arm.

Helen clawed at his face, but he grabbed her, pinning her arms to her side. Her breasts rubbed against his rough-spun uniform shirt as he dragged her out of the water.

"Yeah, bring her right up here," the man said, his hand off his cock and reaching out for her. He grabbed her upper arm, calloused fingers closing around like steel cables. "You like to hit?" He asked, punching her in the stomach.

White fire burned in Helen's gut as she fought to breathe. She was pushed down, wet earth and rocks dug into her back. The man wrapped his hands around her throat, smacking her skull against the river stones. Helen was fading to black, watching his face change as she began to pass out. His penis brushed her pubic hair, leaving a string of clear fluid.

In a spray of warm blood and chunks of flesh, he was gone. At least his head was. His decapitated corpse stayed erect for just a moment before toppling sideways into the dirt. The man's penis softened as his lifeblood gushed from the bloody stump above his shoulders.

"No, please. It wasn't my idea. I wasn't going to do anything," Otis cried.

Helen was still dazed but saw another pair of feet in front of her. Otis was on the ground cowering. He'd shit his pants.

Helen's gaze wandered to the other man's decapitated corpse. It wasn't neat like a surgeon's, no, this one was brutal. Tendons, sinew, and bone poked out of the stump left on the corpse of the would-be rapist. She looked at Otis, who was trying to backpedal from the person in front of him. A shadow in the shape of a man fell on Otis, his mouth latching onto his neck and ripping. Flesh tore like fabric and a wet slurping sound cut through the night.

Helen's head felt six sizes too big and was throbbing. She even forgot she was naked and in front of a stranger. She watched as the man, at least she thought it was a man, let go of Otis, who was dead at this point. Otis's youthful face was locked in a perpetual gaze of fear. His neck was bitten nearly to his spine and meat and gristle shone in the light of the full moon.

The stranger's mouth looked like a shark, full of nasty teeth and covered in blood.

He smiled at her, at least that's what her fear-addled brain thought. It was predatory, but...inviting.

He moved.

Helen wanted to put her hands up to defend herself, but he was so damn fast.

SARIN JUMPED UP, her hands in front of her as if pushing someone away.

"Your birth dream again?" Vee-Exx asked, sitting by a blacked-out window in the small bedroom of the camper.

Sarin looked around, her dead heart quivering in her husk of a chest. She put a cold hand to it.

"Yeah," she said, sitting up on the bed. "Now that was a wild night."

"At least your birth was eventful," Vee said, jumping back into the bed, putting her cold body against Sarin. "Mine was pretty straightforward."

Sarin turned to look at her. She brushed her hair out of her face so she could better see the vampire next to her.

"Now listen here, I saved your ass too."

Vee sat up on her elbows. Her spiky, green hair made her look like a Troll.

"I was just fine until you interjected."

Sarin laughed. "Oh, really? You had a gunshot wound in your gut. You would've died in that alley if I hadn't come along."

The Roaring 20s roared a little too loud for Vee, formally known as Jessica Fontaine. She was a classic case of 'the wrong place at the wrong time' and was hit by a stray bullet in a drive-by shooting in Chicago. Sarin, or Helen O'Shea as she was known back then, found her in the alley; black liver blood seeping from her wound. Normally she would've fed and left, but Sarin saw something in the skinny, tall girl. Something great.

"Yeah, and the rest is history," Vee said, staring into Sarin's eyes.

"Come on, let's check on Nic," Sarin said, getting up from the bed. She pounded on the door. "Are we good?" She asked, not wanting to open the door, getting a face full of fatal sunlight.

"Yeah, come on up," Nic yelled from the driver's seat.

Sarin looked at Vee, her hand on the door handle. "We have to die sometime."

Vee chuckled, "We already did."

Sarin opened the door into the darkness.

Nic sat behind the wheel in front. The headlights cut through the darkness ahead of them, carving a path.

Sarin walked up, holding onto the table to keep her balance. "Where are we?" she asked.

Nic looked at the GPS and said, "Somewhere in bumblefuck, but we need gas and there's a truck stop not far."

"Good, I need to stretch my legs," Vee said, joining them.

Sarin patted Nic on the shoulder, like a good dog. "Ok, stop when you need to. I want to make this next gig on time."

"Aye, aye, captain," Nic said, saluting the dashboard.

THE TRUCK STOP WAS HUGE, as most of them tended to be. Massive fuel pumps were spread out. Large 'diesel' signs lit up the night as bugs crashed to their deaths in the neon glow. Long, numbered parking spaces were lined up along the back of the lot, not many were full. A smaller fuel island was lit, this one selling unleaded gas, instead of diesel.

Nic pulled the camper up to one of the unleaded pumps. He looked at it, getting the number off it.

"Are you coming in?" he asked Vee and Sarin.

"Yeah. I need to walk a little, take in some new smells. This place is getting stale," Vee said, putting on a pair of round lens sunglasses. She wasn't a *Beatles* fan, but loved the John Lennon style glasses. Even though it was night, the bright lights still bothered their eyes. If it was sunlight, no amount of UV protection would save them. They'd be dead; burned to a crisp in seconds.

Sarin put on a tight, black jean jacket. Just a little something to accessorize her outfit. She pulled her pair of shades out, black aviators, and slid them onto her face. She grabbed a tube of black lipstick and freshened up.

"How do I look?" she asked Vee, pursing her full lips. This was one of those times she would've loved to be able to use a mirror.

Vee lowered her glasses and stared. "Mmm, good enough to eat," she said, licking her lips.

"Ah, hello," Nic said, poking his head back into the vehicle. "Let's go. I have to piss and I want to fill this thing up."

Sarin laughed. "Mortals. They always think they're running out of time," she opened the door on the side of the camper, holding it for Vee.

"That's because they are," Vee said, shutting the door behind her. She left it unlocked purposely. If someone broke in, it would make things much easier. They wouldn't even have to hunt. On cue, Vee's stomach growled.

"I know. I'm getting hungry too," Sarin said, her hand rubbing her flat stomach.

Nic walked into the gas station's store. It was a common sight in America and almost everything was laid out the same way. Fresh coffee and pre-wrapped pastries by the door, along with racks of books, newspapers, and magazines. Rows of snacks ranging from salty, sweet, savory, and even some exotic jerky. The beverage coolers lined the wall, each glowing with cold product.

It all looked like shit to Vee and Sarin. Their taste buds had a peculiar attraction and it wasn't found on the shelves. But it was found in the store.

Men, mostly heavyset, pasty and with a breathing problem, lingered around. Some glanced at them, while others outright glared.

Sarin pulled a magazine from the rack and began perusing it. Her dark glasses hid her eyes as she took in the livestock.

Vee tapped her on the shoulder, holding something up. "Should we get them?" She held a pair of novelty vampire fangs. The cheap, plastic-hinged ones that would choke you when you were a kid.

Sarin laughed, looking at the brand name. "Spooky Noodle Novelty, huh. Well, Mr. Noodle, you don't know dick." She grinned at Vee.

Vee set the teeth down on a random rack. "See anything good?" Vee asked, standing next to her.

Nic ran up to the counter and grabbed the bathroom key, which was attached to a fly swatter. He disappeared around the corner by the drink coolers.

"I think so, but I don't think we're going to have to work very hard for it."

Sarin's gaze, hidden by tinted glass, fell on two men, both of whom were staring at her and Vee.

"Fucking lesbos probably," the one in a ripped, blaze orange jacket said.

"Yeah, but I'd pay a pretty penny to see that show," the other, this one in a blue jumpsuit, reminiscent of Michael Myers. He absently rubbed his crotch, eyeing the two women.

"Na, too skinny for me," Orange Jacket said. He licked his lips. "Probably fucking whores anyway. Crack whores. I mean, who the fuck else dyes their hair green and wears fucking sunglasses at night? Do these skanks think they're Johnny fucking Cash?"

Michael Myers started laughing. "If they are whores, they'll make a whole lot of money. I'll be their first customer." He kept rubbing himself, the bulge getting larger.

"Too fucking easy," Vee whispered. "Watch this."

"I always do," Sarin said, her dead eyes on the men.

"Do you pencil dicks have something to say? We can hear you, ya know," she stared at them trying to be intimidating. She was tall for a woman, but her thin frame was nothing for the fat-covered slabs of muscle both men were lugging around.

"What did you call me, you fucking skank?" Orange Jacket said, putting the package of cupcakes back on the shelf.

"Hard of hearing?" Sarin said. "Is that from your pencil-dick daddy fucking your ears when you were a boy?" She put a black-nailed finger to her lips. "Or maybe he fucked your little ass. Not sure, but he's definitely been inside you."

His face turned red and blotchy as he started over towards her. "Listen here, you fucking cunt, don't you dare disrespect my daddy! Don't you fucking dare!"

He was close to her. Close enough Sarin could hear the elevated sound of his pulse. The slight shudder in his neck as his blood pressure rose. She wanted to lick her lips thinking about ripping his throat out in the store, but she knew it would have to wait.

"Hey, what's going on?" Nic said, walking up to the tense group.

"Are you these whore's pimp?" Michael Myers asked, joining his friend. His friend's outburst seemed to renew his vigor in harassing women late at night.

"Easy, fellas," Nic said, flashing a smile that had many concertgoers losing their clothes by the end of the night. "We aren't looking for trouble, just passing through to get some fuel. That's it." He had his hands up, showing them he was no threat. If only they knew about Vee and Sarin.

"Hey," the clerk said to the group of them. "Buy something or get out. This isn't a fucking hang out."

"Come on," Michael Myers said, patting Orange Jacket on the arm, "I'm going to turn in before my next haul. You should too."

He shrugged his friend's hand off and pointed at Sarin. "You're lucky, you fucking hear me?"

Sarin ignored him and tried to walk by.

The man grabbed her arm.

"Jesus Christ, you're ice fucking cold," he looked at his hand as if it were covered in bugs. He looked at Sarin and Vee in abhorrent disgust. "Get the fuck away from me," he said, backing away from the vampires. The door chimed as he ran out, heading to his truck.

"Ah, $40 on pump 6," Nic said to the clerk.

"WELL, WHAT DO YOU THINK?" Nic asked, back in the camper and sitting in the back with the vampires. He had two chili dogs in front of him, the third one was already in his stomach. He grabbed his disgustingly large soda and took a sip. With the back of his hand, he stifled a burp.

Sarin looked out the window, one of the ones not blacked out.

Orange Jacket's truck was still parked in the lot and running. She had a feeling he was spending the night. Most of the other trucks had left, leaving none near his.

"We might not get another chance to feed before tomorrow night," Sarin said, mainly to Vee.

"Agreed," Vee said, looking over Sarin's shoulder.

"Ok," Nic said, wiping runny chili from his chin. "Let me finish first, so we can get the fuck out of here when you're done."

"Ok, but hurry up. I'm starving."

LANCE BEAUREGARD, AKA Orange Jacket, lay on his small bed in the sleeper of his truck. He was watching some stupid shit on his phone, knowing he should be sleeping. He couldn't help it. In the past few months, he'd taken so many caffeine pills and speed, he was afraid he permanently fucked up his brain. The blue light from the phone screen was giving him a headache and he finally decided it was time to try and sleep.

His eyes opened. Someone was knocking on his truck.

"Goddamit," he said, pulling back his blanket. He was feeling sleep approaching before the knock. It was probably fucking Earl, seeing if he had any cigarettes. He opened the curtain separating his sleeper compartment from the driver and passenger seat. He looked in the side-view mirror, but didn't see anyone. "What the fuck?" he grumbled, climbing over the passenger seat, the side he thought the sound came from. He opened the door.

Sarin stood there. She'd removed the black jacket and wore

only her tank top. She stole a page out of Vee's playbook and shed the bra. Her breasts hung a little, but they were far from saggy. They had the ideal amount of natural hang and every man told her they were perfect. Well, just before she ate them. Her nipples were at attention and she carried a bottle of whiskey.

Lance wanted to be mad, he did, but one look in those deep, dark eyes and everything changed. Suddenly, he wasn't mad anymore. In fact, he was happy to see her standing at his truck, with what looked like a peace offering in her hands. He was far from a lady's man, at 43 years old, a potbelly that peeked over his beltline, eczema, and a permanent 'salami' smell. Of course, he would fuck lot lizards, the prostitutes that would roam truck stops. Usually, they were more disgusting than him, but he didn't mind. He just wanted a warm hole to put his cock in.

"Look, I'm sorry for before," Sarin said, her one arm hugged tight across her body, feigning being cold. "I want to make it up to you," she said, holding up the bottle.

Lance, who wished he'd paid to use the shower earlier, looked at the young woman. Her black hair framed her pale skin and without her sunglasses, her eyes looked like two chips of obsidian. He was in awe.

"Well, you were out of line," he said, rubbing the back of his neck. Flakes of skin fell down his shirt. "But maybe I was wrong too." He mumbled the last part, hating to admit wrong in any instance. This time it might get him laid by the best-looking woman he'd ever had.

"Can I come in?" Sarin said, waiting patiently for his invite.

"Yes, you can come in," he said.

Sarin smiled, handing him the bottle and grabbing a rail to pull herself up.

"Sorry about the mess," he said, looking at the bottle of booze. "I wasn't expecting company." He shuffled into the driver's seat and pointed to the bed in the back. "Take a seat and

I'll pour us a drink." He said, grabbing two fast food cups that were semi-empty.

Sarin took a seat on the bed, watching him pour the alcohol into the cups.

He took a sip from one, "Hey, this isn't half bad," he said. "I've never had-," he stopped, looking up at the small mirror he kept on the dash. She was a blur. At first, he thought maybe something was on the mirror and then she shifted; the blur moved.

Lance turned, seeing death incarnate. His bladder released just before Sarin attacked.

She'd changed in an instant. Her beautiful, symmetrical face was distorted by her wide mouth and protruding jaw. Rows of shark-like teeth shone in the glow of the neon lights. Sarin's fingers, tipped with dagger-like claws, grabbed Lance by the arm. She pulled, feeling the rewarding pop of his shoulder dislocating. It didn't matter, the muscle and flesh were strong enough to pull him into her waiting maw. Her jaws attached to his throat, easily severing layers of fat and cartilage. The warm, salty release of his lifeblood filled her mouth. It was ecstasy. The tang of sweat on his flesh, the acrid smell of fear, and of course the nourishing iron taste of his blood.

Sarin drank greedily, filling her belly to bursting. She took more.

"Hey, save some for me," Vee said, opening the door. She was waiting outside next to Sarin when Lance invited her in. She jumped into the truck, closing the door behind her. Like the predator she was, she dove into the bloody meal.

8

THE TRUNK

CYRIL AND NESTOR sat in their small living room, with a relic from their past on the coffee table in front of them.

The old trunk, a family heirloom passed down to Visser men for generations, sat open.

Cyril had a heavy revolver in his hand. The cylinder was open and empty. He spun it, the old, and well-used metal hummed. With a deft hand, one that hadn't held a gun in years, he snapped it shut.

"This is it?" Nestor said, pulling a few more items from the trunk. In his hands were a pair of brass knuckles with silver crosses inlaid in them. Silver wasn't fatal to a vampire, but they certainly didn't care for it. He flexed his fingers in the familiar grips of the weapon. He took them off, setting them aside and picked up another revolver. He checked to ensure it was empty, opening the cylinder. His father always taught him firearms safety and knowing the condition of your weapon was important. He put the gun next to the knuckles and pulled out a box of ammunition.

The box was unremarkable. It was plain-looking white cardboard, with a faded red cross on the center of it. It was the only one left and felt light.

Cyril, with his gun in hand, watched his brother. "Are there any more?" He asked, peering into the trunk. He knew there wasn't, but had to look anyway.

"No, these are the only ones left," Nestor showed him the box, which contained 24 rounds of ammo. He closed the box up and set it to the side. "Fuck," he said, rooting around, hoping for maybe a loose round or two. He found none. "It's not like we can just run out and buy them either."

"We should be fine with what we have," Cyril reached across his brother and picked up the box of rounds. He opened it, taking one out.

The bullets were rare. Not only rare but special order. Most people thought vampires could only be killed by a wooden stake in the heart, but as generations of Vissers knew, this was a lie. The only true way to kill a vampire was with fire, but not any fire. The fire, or the fuel for the fire, needed to contain holy water from the river Jordan. Then and only then, would the flames purify the unholy beasts, destroying them. Over the generations, Cyril and Nestor's ancestors found other ways to injure or weaken a vampire, such as the blessed bullets. Each bullet was carefully handcrafted, the molten lead mixed with holy water and blessed by a pure priest. These bullets would injure and weaken the vampire, making them easier to set ablaze. If not, they were unnaturally fast and agile.

Nestor looked at his brother examining the round. He hoped they would be ok. Ever since their father had died neither of them had so much as been in a fistfight. Sure, a few of their targets in the PI work had gotten upset, but nothing was ever too physical. A shoving match here and there was about the extent of it. Now they were out to hunt not one, but two, possibly three vampires.

They didn't know much about them either, which made it all

the more difficult. Some vampires were babies, only born during this generation. They hadn't perfected their glamor skills or hunter's instincts. Those were easy kills and could usually be tricked, shot, and burned. No, they had no way of knowing if these vampires were 30 years old or 300 years old. There weren't too many 300-year-old vampires left, especially in the United States. Their father had told them of a great assault on some of the oldest vampires in the country that had taken place in the 70s. Many vampire hunters were killed, but an entire brood of vampires, their creator being 230 years old, were wiped out.

Since talking with John, the two brothers were on a mission, one they didn't take lightly. They did some research on the band, thank the gods of the internet for making it so easy. There wasn't much on them, but it was enough. They had a few sparse social media pages, but they only used them to announce shows. That was fine with Nestor, who began cross-referencing the show locations with any murders or disappearances within fifty miles.

He didn't come away empty-handed. All over the country, bodies turned up. They were mangled and mutilated, looking like they'd been attacked by wild animals. Most of the medical examiners chalked it up to that. Not only because of the extent of the wounds but for the sheer fact, not a single trace of DNA was ever recovered. Not even a stray hair, which was odd in the case of animal attacks. The MEs knew open cases would lead to questions and questions, regardless of how good you were, you were never good enough. Besides, their agencies didn't like unsolved cases, so if a wild dog, mountain lion, or bear could be blamed, so be it.

This didn't get past Nestor and Cyril, no. They knew what they were looking for. City by city, they tracked the band. And city by city, the corpses piled up.

Nestor patted his brother on the shoulder, looking him in the eyes.

Cyril always looked more like their father and Nestor their mother.

"I fucking hope so. I hope we still got it."

Cyril smiled at him, that award-winning smile that had led many men to his bed.

"We'll be fine." He stood, pointing his gun at the wall. "Hell, we're Vissers." He pulled the hammer back and dry-fired the gun with a click.

Nestor wished he could echo his brother's enthusiasm and confidence, but couldn't. It just didn't feel right to him without their father there. He forced a smile, noticing Cyril was looking at him. This job was life-changing. That amount of money could do wonders for them, propelling their business further than ever dreamed.

Nestor began repacking the trunk. "You're right. We're going to kill these unholy fucks, get paid and —,"

"Get laid," Cyril said, laughing at his lame joke. "Sorry, it was too perfect not to."

Nestor smiled, this one in earnest. "Come on, I want to hit the road soon. We need to beat them there."

Cyril handed his brother the gun and it was replaced in its proper spot, keeping it safe.

"Alright, let's roll."

9

THE HOPE THEY GIVE

Nɪᴄ and the vampires drove through the night and into the morning. Once the murderous rays of golden sun rose in the east, the vampires had already been locked away in their blacked-out room for an hour.

Nic didn't mind driving alone and after five years, he'd gotten used to it. His only issue was trying to maintain their sleep schedule. When he was right out of high school, he picked up a warehouse job loading trucks. He'd been stuck on overnights and would have to teach his body to sleep in the daytime. At 18 years old, this wasn't a problem, but now it seemed to drain him. He had some tricks of the trade, but sleeping when everyone else was awake could be odd.

He looked at his GPS. They were less than thirty miles from the venue where they were playing later that night. It was as good a time as any to find a spot to park the camper for the day and get some rest.

The two vampires squealed in their room and he thought maybe they weren't quite ready for sleep yet either. He knew this wouldn't happen; they rarely opened that door during the day for anything. Besides, they sounded like they were having plenty of fun without him.

Nic shook his head, warding off the nods, and saw a sight for sore eyes up ahead. A sign for an old mini-mall was crossed out, a realtor's sign diagonally across it. He checked his side mirror, making sure no one was behind him, and slowed down.

The mini-mall was empty. All of the storefronts were depressingly boarded up and if not, their windows were shattered.

Nic, the ever-cautious and responsible driver, put his blinker on, guiding the vehicle into the parking lot. Rocks, weeds, bottles, cigarette butts and packs, all fell victim to the tires of the camper. He began driving towards the side of the building, hoping to get around back, hiding the vehicle. Massive, solid jersey barriers blocked his way. They were bright yellow and covered in the vilest graffiti he'd ever seen. He spun the camper around, parking it as close to the side of the building as possible. It would have to do.

He killed the engine, grabbed his smokes and phone, and hopped out. Nic stretched, the smell of his armpits hitting his nose. He desperately needed a shower. Maybe after the show, he'd refill the water tank on the camper. The water heater didn't work, but a cold shower was better than nothing.

He had his sunglasses on his forehead and pulled them down over his eyes, blocking out some of the glaring rays. He leaned on the warm hood, put a cigarette in his mouth and took out his phone. He puffed away, hoping to get the nicotine into his blood so he could sleep. His setup wasn't nearly as good as Sarin and Vee's, but it was ok. Above the driver and passenger seats was a loft-style bunk. There was a folding ladder he could use to get up, but he just pulled himself up. It wasn't much, but it was better than the floor.

Nic finished his smoke, tossing it on the cracked blacktop to join the hundreds of others. He turned to walk back to the driver's side and stopped.

A sound halted him. The sound of a car pulling into the lot.

CAMERON DROVE THROUGH THE NIGHT. He stopped once for a power nap when he nearly sideswiped the guardrail. Besides that 20-minute nap, he hadn't slept. His body was full of emotions.

Shame, embarrassment, guilt, anger and hope. He was ashamed and embarrassed for sending that stupid pic. He knew better than that. It was one of the worst decisions of his life. He fucking hated all of them, Tara included. She was supposed to be different, better than them. She had to do what was needed to fit in, but fucking humiliate him like that? No, that was uncalled for. Even though his mother was a drunken whore, he felt a twinge of guilt about leaving her. Plus, he'd taken any bit of money he could find. It wasn't much, but it was hers. She'd have to suck and fuck extra to get her booze. His anger had subsided, but not completely. When he saw Pat's post, he wanted to kill him. In his mind at that moment, he related with every school shooter who was bullied. He wanted to see their fear as he walked through the halls of his school, the Angel of Fucking Death, pumping hollow point after hollow point into each of them. To see them fall, and bleed. Crying for him to stop and they were sorry, just before he finished them. Maybe he'd use a knife to finish them off after shooting them? That would've been a great idea. Feel their life ebb from them through a blade. He probably would even make Tara strip. She wanted to play fucking games with him, he'd play with her. If he didn't think there was something else for him, school on Monday would've been a bad day for a lot of them.

After Cameron left the apartment, he'd been in a whirlwind of pain, but there was something else there; hope. It was only a faint glimmer, but it was there. He didn't know if the vampires would accept him and highly doubted it, but he played the scenarios over and over in his head.

Maybe they'd see something in him. Maybe they were looking for another member. Even if he had to stay human for the time being, he would if they'd make him into a vampire eventually. He knew it was a pipe dream, something that would never happen, but he held out hope. If he didn't, he would've pulled over and blown his brains out with his dad's 1911.

Cameron drove on, the hope outweighing his need for sleep. The roads seemed to blend together. The lines faded and each reflector looked like oncoming headlights. Once daylight broke, he knew he'd get a second wind. At least he thought so. Sleep was winning and he was starting to fade, knowing he needed to stop soon or he'd crash, never making it to the show.

A sign for a mini-mall was up ahead. He looked, noticing a realtor's sign covered most of it. He slowed down, scanning the lot and nearly crashed at what he saw.

An unmistakable black camper with red letters of *AGOD* on the side, sat parked near the building.

Cameron's heart smashed against his ribcage. Adrenaline surged through his bloodstream, waking him up in an instant. Was this his chance? He didn't know, but he couldn't let it go to waste. At least he had to introduce himself, maybe make contact with the male drummer, who was certainly human. Obviously, the vampires, Vee-Exx and Sarin, wouldn't be out in the daytime. At least that's what every bit of vampire lore said.

Without thinking twice, Cameron turned into the lot. His tires popped and crunched over debris. He saw someone standing outside the camper. It was the drummer, Arsenic.

Cameron drove on auto-pilot, not knowing what the hell he

was going to say. He stopped his car by the camper and got out. He knew he looked like microwaved shit; crying earlier in the night, no sleep, and nothing to eat in hours. He didn't care, this was his chance.

"Hi," Cameron croaked, his throat dry. He gathered spit, swallowing it down, hoping to lube his vocal cords. "I'm Cameron," he said to Arsenic, who stood not responding.

NIC WATCHED the shitbox car pull up and stop. He could see what appeared to be a teenage boy in the driver's seat. He looked like a metal head, with his dark clothes, overall unhealthy skin, and shitty beard. When he stepped out wearing some unreadable black metal hoodie, Nic knew he was just dealing with a fan. He probably wanted an autograph or maybe a picture of the camper. It wasn't uncommon. Nic would oblige and send him on his way.

"Hi," the kid paused, seeming to swallow hard, "I'm Cameron."

Nic didn't move to shake the kid's hand, just stood watching. He took out another cigarette. He figured if he was going to stand outside any longer, he might as well get another smoke in.

"Arsenic, but just call me Nic," Nic said, lighting his cigarette.

Cameron smiled, toeing a bottle cap on the ground. He had a hard time keeping eye contact with Nic, and didn't know how he was going to do the next part.

"Pleasure to meet you, Nic. I love your music." Cameron said, looking at the black windows on the back half of the camper.

Nic noticed the boy looking at the windows, but didn't say anything. He took a drag of his cigarette, watching the boy through the cloud of smoke.

"Thanks. We have a show tonight." Nic said, looking at his phone, which he'd pulled out, trying to give the hint to 'get the fuck away from me'. "I'm actually about to go get some rest, so I'm ready." He flicked the butt, it landed in a shower of sparks.

"I know, I'll be there," Cameron said, his eyes following the flying cigarette butt.

"Alright then, I'll see you tonight," Nic said, walking towards the door of the camper.

Cameron's mind was racing. This was his chance. His only chance. He felt like he'd eaten a bucket of slugs and worms. It was almost as bad as the feeling he had earlier when he saw the picture of his genitals on the internet.

"Wait," Cameron yelled, reaching out as if he was going to grab Nic, who was nowhere near him.

Nic stopped and turned. He sucked his teeth in annoyance. He wanted to fucking sleep.

"I want to join you," Cameron blurted out.

Nic scrunched his face up. "No thanks, kid. Our band is full," he turned to walk away.

"No," Cameron said. "I want to be a vampire."

This stopped Nic in his tracks. He did his best to maintain his composure and didn't turn around until he'd taken a few deep breaths.

"Yeah, good one, kid. Not all death metal bands are into the occult and shit." He waved his hand. "Now, fucking beat it. I need some rest." Nic's heart was pounding. Since he'd been with the band, it was rare for anyone to actually call them out.

Cameron took a step forward. He was glistening with sweat on his forehead.

"No, well can you explain these?" Cameron started rattling off missing persons and unsolved murder cases around the nation.

Nic felt sick and wished it was after dark so Vee and Sarin could handle this punk-ass kid.

"Look, kid," Nic put his hands up. They shook slightly. "I'm done entertaining your crazy, fucking ideas. There are no boogeymen or vampires here. It's all an act, ok. We're performers, who perform. That's it." Nic, who was shaking with an adrenaline dump, walked away. This time, he wouldn't turn around.

CAMERON WATCHED NIC WALK AWAY. He knew he'd gotten to him and that was enough.

Nic disappeared around the side of the camper, opening the door and vanishing inside. The tell-tale sound of locks being thrown echoed off the abandoned buildings.

Cameron stared at the camper for a second longer and decided there was nothing more he could do. The show was later that night and he'd try again, this time under the cover of darkness, hopefully being able to talk with the actual vampires.

He was quivering, but elated. The reaction of Nic solidified the fact the other members of the band were in fact vampires. Cameron knew it all along, but this was the proof he needed.

Cameron walked back to his car and started it up. He put it in drive and left the lot, running over more trash on the way out. He'd find another place to sleep; he'd be seeing them later, that was for sure.

NIC GOT BACK into the driver's seat of the camper, sliding behind the wheel. Normally he would've taken the gun he kept in between the seats, but he didn't expect to be hunted down by a kid. Lesson learned. He'd be grabbing the gun whenever he left the camper.

"Fuck," he said, trying not to be loud. He didn't know if Sarin and Vee were asleep or not. This wasn't a problem, but he knew it could be. Sure, this kid wasn't the first to discover them. It'd happened time and time again, but usually, it was a drunk fan, who figured they were vampires by their songs or clothes. Those were easy. They'd play to them for a little while and if the vampires thought they'd make a decent meal; they were invited in for a drink. No, this kid was nervous but had an air of confidence about him unlike any of the others. He knew something, something concrete.

"Nic," one of the vampires called from the bedroom. They weren't asleep.

"Yeah."

"What was that about?" One of them asked. He wasn't sure, but he thought it was Sarin.

Nic thought about lying but knew better. When he'd first joined up with them, he told them a lie. It was the last one he'd ever uttered, especially anywhere near their presence. Their hearing was unnaturally good, and he had no idea of the actual range on it.

"Just a kid," he said, not a lie, but not nearly the truth. He knew this was an act; they'd heard everything.

"Put the blinders up," this voice was Sarin. "Then come in, but quickly. You know the rules."

Nic did know the rules. The vampires would rarely open their little bedroom sanctuary during the day, but if they did certain measures needed to be in place first. Nic had to cover the windshield and all windows with heavy, black cloth. The only sunlight visible was just a slight glow on the edges of the fabric.

Nic moved around with a practiced hand, covering everything. Gloom settled on the interior of the camper. He found a light switch and flipped it on. The interior of the camper lit up in red; the lone red bulb tucked next to a white one in the ceiling.

"Ok, we're blacked out," he said, walking the few steps to the bedroom door. He heard them shuffling around inside.

"Come in," Vee said.

Nic grabbed the handle and pushed the door open just wide enough for him to slip through.

The room was lit red.

Sarin lay on the bed, her back propped up against the wall. She was nude, her pale skin bathed in blood-red light. Her light nipples took on an angry shade of crimson. Vee's face was buried in her crotch. The sounds of her lapping at Sarin's pussy were almost hypnotic.

Sarin stared at Nic; her fingers entwined in Vee's short hair. Gently, she controlled the placement of the other vampire's probing tongue. She kept her eyes locked on Nic's, purring as she thrust her mound hard against Vee's face.

Nic had seen this thousands of times and loved every one. This was a perk, but also a fear. When Vee and Sarin were aroused and fully enraptured with sex, it was amazing. It could also be lethal. He'd seen them go from wild sex to ravenous monsters in seconds. Since he was the only human there, if they decided he was finally on the menu, there was nothing he could do. It still didn't stop him from getting hard.

"About the kid," he said, watching Sarin's eyes roll back in pleasure.

"Oh, we don't fucking care. We heard it all from in here."

"Yeah, he's nothing," Vee said, taking her face from Sarin's wet cunt. Her chin glistening in the glow of the red bulb. "But you," she said, licking her lips. She reached out and pulled him close to the bed. Within seconds, Nic's pants were off.

The first time he was inside of their cold bodies, it felt odd. The friction of rough sex warmed them up enough, but there was nothing like a live girl.

Vee expertly worked him, showing her oral sex skills were not just reserved for females.

Nic closed his eyes in bliss, thinking, *'If I have to die, there are certainly worse ways to go.'* He kicked his leg out, shutting the door.

10

GRANNY BANGER

CYRIL AND NESTOR checked into the cheap motel with cash and fake IDs. They'd been to enough seedy places to know a good one. The lobby was tinged with a cloud of cigarette smoke. The walls had wallpaper from three generations ago and the carpet wasn't much better. It appeared to have, at one time, a pattern, but now it was ripped and the yellow color of fat. A lone vending machine sat humming in the corner. They didn't have to read expiration dates to know nothing was fresh in that thing.

The clerk was a woman in her mid-50's, Peg Bundy hair and a smoker's cough that sounded like she'd inhaled glass. She didn't even look at the IDs, which are decent fakes. Cyril was annoyed. He spent good money on them and they didn't even get properly examined.

The woman put her cigarettes down and turned down the small TV she had on the counter. She looked up at them with an accusing glare.

"What brings you boys to our neck of the woods?" She asked, tucking her cigarette back into her mouth. Plum-colored lips wrapped around the filter, causing more wrinkles to crease in her face. She pulled deeply, never taking her eyes off them.

Nestor grabbed the key, which she had slid across the counter. He turned on the charm, staring at her as if she were a pert, high-breasted, tight box 18-year-old cheerleader. Not a washed-up hag, who probably had a cunt looking like hairy elephant ears.

The clerk smiled, her ice gaze melting. Smoke flowed from her upturned mouth and nose.

"Why, ma'am, we're just passing through. We'll be out of your lovely hair by the morning." Nestor said, leaning on the counter.

Cyril rolled his eyes so obviously it was almost audible.

This woman, who had it out for them thirty seconds prior, was melting for Nestor's bullshit charm.

"But," Nestor leaned closer, gesturing for her to come forward, "if you really want to find out, come up to the room in an hour." He winked at her, backing away from the stench of smoke coming from her breath.

She was his. She smiled and blushed like the first time she'd been kissed.

"Well, I don't think that is appropriate at all," she said, still grinning ear to ear. She touched her well-sprayed hair, making sure it had the proper amount of body. "But I do get off in two hours if that's ok?"

Nestor hoisted his duffle bag onto his shoulder. "I'll see you in two," he said before walking back outside.

"What the fuck?" Cyril asked, watching his brother look for their room.

Nestor headed up a flight of dilapidated stairs checking the doors. Most of them had numbers, but some didn't. He asked for a very specific room, so hopefully they were getting close.

"What?" Nestor asked, stopping outside of a door with no

numbers. It was between 214 and 216, so his best guess was this door was their room, 215.

"That thing, with the old hag," Cyril said, gesturing below them towards the office.

Nestor put the key in, having to jiggle the knob to get the lock to disengage.

"Oh, come on, I was just having fun," Nestor smirked, pushing the door in.

The room was clean but severely outdated. Two twin beds sat nice and neatly made, with two, wafer-thin pillows at their heads. The bedspreads had a floral pattern on them, perfect for hiding stains.

"Really?" Cyril said, yanking the bedspread off the bed and onto the floor.

Nestor looked at him with a questioning glance.

"These fucking things are nasty." He said, looking at the top sheet. It was bleached white, putting him at ease. "Do you know how much cum gets shot on these things?" He asked. "Trust me, I do, so, eww no." He put his bag on the bed. "Anyway, what the fuck are you going to do if she comes up here?"

Nestor, taking his brother's advice, removed the bedspread. He knew what fluids of his had been on them, so he thought the removal was sound advice.

"I'm not sure yet," he smiled at his brother. He hadn't done much research on any new fetishes since he gave Annette Ryerson a Roman Shower of his vomit. "Maybe I'll just fuck her. You know, good ole sex." He put his finger to his lips in thought. "I wonder how old she is? Gerontophilia is something I haven't done yet."

Cyril was making mock gagging noises.

"Oh, come on," Nestor said, pulling the large revolver from his duffle bag. It was empty, but he checked it over. "I've seen some of the dudes you bring back and some aren't so pretty."

Cyril tilted his head and pursed his lips. "Yeah, ok, but I'm not fucking some dried-up, old woman."

Nestor smiled and flicked his tongue out like a snake. "I know how to get her wet."

"Barf," Cyril said, pulling his weapons out. "Anyway, Granny Banger, why this room?"

Nestor put his gun back in the bag and gestured for Cyril to do the same. He walked over to the window and pulled back the polyester shade. "There," he said pointing through the smudged glass.

Cyril looked at the row of buildings. The last one in the row bordered a large parking lot. He knew what it was from the pictures online.

"That's the venue, isn't it?" He asked, already knowing the answer.

"Yes, *Shades* is the name of it," Nestor said, letting the curtain close. "Their show starts at 9:00 pm, so I want us to be set and ready." Nestor began pulling more stuff from his bag. "I'm hoping to get in, catch them in the camper, torch them with cleansing fire and get the fuck out. Just another couple of concert-goers caught in the tragedy of young lives snuffed out."

"What about witnesses?" Cyril asked, sitting down at the small table in the room. The chair wobbled. "What if we have to fire a few rounds to bring them down before torching them?" A concerned look shot across his face. "What if they leave?"

Nestor thought about that on the way over. There was a very good chance gunfire would be involved. If the vampires knew they were coming or knew something was awry, they would come out fighting. In that case, the brothers would have to resort to using their holy rounds to weaken the beasts and then setting them ablaze. Neither man wanted it that way, but they had to prepare. If they left, the brothers would follow them. They would hunt them to the ends of the earth.

"That might happen. If so, shoot fast, burn'em and we'll get the fuck out of Dodge." This was easier said than done. With the chaos of gunfire and a burning camper, onlookers would be everywhere. Their only option was to be ready to get in the car and drive the fuck out. If the cops caught them, they'd have some explaining to do. "Let's hope not. If they leave, we follow and wait for our chance. We're Visser's, vampire killing is in our blood." Nestor took out a small bottle of holy water. "Go to the store and get a few iced teas in glass bottles and a gallon of gas." He held the holy liquid, blessed water from the River Jordan, up to his face. "The purifying fire of God will rid the world of these monsters."

LAST MEAL

CAMERON WOKE WITH A START. He jumped, banging his knees on the steering wheel of his car. He was hot, sticky, and smelled like a bag of onions.

The dream, the dread of the night his father was killed, coated him like grease. His entire body felt slick with sin.

He steadied his nerves, rubbing his face to calm down. Finally, the nightmare began to ebb away, even though that night would never leave him. His mouth tasted vile and he wondered if he'd secretly eaten a stink bug while he slept. Cameron grabbed a bottle of water and rinsed his mouth. He swallowed the tepid liquid, giving some relief to his dry throat.

The sun was setting, just visible through the trees.

After leaving the mini-mall parking lot, Cameron drove another ten minutes or so before the urge to sleep hit him like a shotgun blast. An access road was the first bit of privacy he could find and carefully tucked his car into the shady spot. He didn't know if he could sleep in the car, even with the seats back. He found out he could and slept hard.

Cameron started the car up, noticing he still had almost 3

hours before the show started. He was starving and hoped there was something decent in town to eat.

It was going to be his last meal.

SARIN WATCHED NIC SLEEP.

He was mumbling, his mouth moving as his body twitched here and there. The dream he was having, one he'd had plenty of times before, started great. The three of them rutting like wild animals. The heat of his living body, mixed with the cold of their undead ones. It started great but didn't end so well for poor Nic. Sarin and Vee decided his time had come and just as his orgasm was reaching its peak, they attacked. The two vampires ripped into his soft, warm flesh, releasing nourishing blood into their fanged mouths.

Sarin ran a black fingernail down his stubbled cheek, loving the hissing sound it made along the way.

Nic's eyes shot open and he scrambled back in his small bunk above the front seats.

Sarin smiled, her teeth looking oh so human and perfectly square.

"Get up," she said, stepping down from the small folding ladder he used to climb up. "We have to get going soon."

Nic looked around, realizing the vampires weren't about to kill him. The camper was dark, only lit by one red light. He rubbed his face and pulled out his phone, checking the time. It was almost 7:30 pm and the show was starting at 9. They weren't the opening act, but they were far from the closers. Besides, they wanted to get there early to look around, see if any human cattle looked promising. Nic climbed down the small ladder and folded it back up.

"Just let me take a leak and have a smoke first and then we'll hit the road."

Vee looked at him from the table. She had a knife in her hand. The tip stuck into the cheap Formica of the tabletop as she twisted it.

"Don't be long," she said, watching him. "That disgusting trucker wasn't enough and I'm getting hungry again." She forced a smile.

Nic grabbed a hoodie and threw it on. Learning his lesson from before, he grabbed the small handgun in between the seats and stuffed it into the front of his pants.

The night air wasn't cold, but there was a chill to it. He could hardly remember what state they were in, let alone the seasons. If he had to guess, it was early Fall; hot in the day, and hoodie weather at night.

Nic popped a cigarette into his mouth, lighting it. He unzipped and listened as the steady flow of piss splashed on the pavement.

The kid from earlier had him shaken up, something he wasn't used to. Usually, Sarin and Vee handled all the muscle work, but he sometimes had to step in. He couldn't put his finger on it, but there was something up with that kid. He knew too much.

"Shake it off and let's fucking go," Sarin said, poking her head out the driver's door.

The last few drops of urine hit the ground and Nic zipped up. He tossed the cigarette butt in the puddle and hopped back in.

"Alright already. Let's get this show on the road," he started the camper.

Nic guided the camper into the parking lot.

Other campers, vans, trucks, and trailers were spread out. Pieces of equipment were laying near the vehicles. Band members and some roadies mingled with each other, as they waited their turn to play. Of course, where there were musicians, there were groupies.

Groupies were the shooting-fish-in-a-barrel fuck. They would linger around backstage, hoping for a chance to fuck or suck a band member (lead singers were their first targets, but guitar players weren't far behind). Even smaller bands, like this show, had their fair share of young women and some men, looking to have a good story the next day.

Most of the meals had by Sarin and Vee were groupies and that night would hopefully be no different.

From inside the venue, loud, violent, and brutal music began vibrating the walls.

The show had started.

———

CYRIL AND NESTOR, now dressed in black t-shirts and jeans, bought tickets at the booth.

"I can't fucking believe we had to pay to listen to that noise," Cyril said from outside the building. They hadn't even walked into the show and he already hated the music.

"All part of the act, brother," Nestor said, scanning the line of waiting patrons.

They all looked the same; pasty skin, black clothes with obscene or obscure band names, dark hair, make-up, and a ton of piercings.

The brothers walked around outside, pretending to look for their car, which was safely parked in an alley a block over. Even though the motel was within walking distance, they had no intentions of going back there. The car was loaded with their weapons and holy relics, including the cleansing firebombs they made. They wished they could have some kind of weapon inside, but security was doing a decent job with the metal detector and pat-downs. They might've had a chance to sneak something in, but it wasn't worth the risk.

Nestor stopped, acting as casual as possible. He pulled his cell phone out, putting it up to his ear as if taking a call.

"There, behind me," he said to Cyril, who was looking at his phone screen.

Cyril opened the camera app on his phone and put it on selfie mode. This allowed him to look behind him without turning around.

"That's them alright," Cyril said, looking at the black camper through his camera. "God, you'd think they'd travel inconspicuously." He locked his screen and put his hands in his pockets. "Fuck, it's chilly," he said, stamping his feet.

"Yup, I know," Nestor said, still pretending to talk on his phone. He shook his head a few times and pressed the screen before putting the phone in his pocket. "Well, we know they're here," he said, walking back towards the main entrance of the venue. "Now, we wait and pray." He and Cyril held up wristbands, showing they'd already paid, and walked in. They were each patted down; Cyril enjoying his a little too much.

The music was deafening. The band on stage beat their instruments like they hated them. Bodies, clothed in black and smelling like cigarettes and sweat, were packed tight. In front of the stage, which was no more than fifty feet from the entrance, a crowd of people were attacking the shit out of each other. Cyril and Nestor knew what a mosh pit was, but had never seen one in real life.

"I need a fucking drink!" Cyril shouted in his brother's ear.

Nestor couldn't hear him, pointing to his ear.

Cyril pointed at the bar, which was currently not too busy.

Nestor held up one finger, hoping to stop his brother from getting drunk. If they were going to be in a fight for their lives, they needed to be sober. Well, mostly sober.

CAMERON WALKED into the venue and felt at peace. The loud, assaultive music battered his eardrums to a blissful humming. The band on stage was good. Their lead guitar was playing one of the most aggressive and fast solos he'd heard in a long time.

He arrived at the show before it started and just kind of drove around. He drove and thought. Thought about everything: his mother, school, the death of his father, the scumbag kids at school, and ultimately, his death. In that drive, he knew his mind was made up. After tonight he'd be dead. Whether it was by his hand or the hands of the vampires, his life would end. He came to the conclusion them welcoming him and just taking him as a vampire was a fucking long shot. About as long of a shot as Tara actually sending him nudes. He didn't care, he just wanted it to end. No more worrying about being picked on in school. No more going to bed hungry and hoping to God you got to school early enough to get breakfast. No more crying in bed, thinking of the night your father died and how your mother, who was fucking God only knew in the next room, blamed you. No, death couldn't be worse than living with bugs, in filth and rot, smelling that sweet, yet putrid odor of trash.

When Cameron decided he'd had enough driving, he went back to the venue. He smiled as a black camper with red lettering came driving in.

Cameron walked up to the bar and ordered water. Usually, he could get drinks, even underage, but he didn't want to risk it. He stepped to the side, letting two guys step up next to him to order their drinks.

Cameron sipped his water, which tasted like chlorine, and tried not to spill it as he was jostled.

The band on stage was winding down and he hoped *A Gift of Death* was next.

He was right.

Nic, with the help of venue staff and a couple of roadies, set up his drums. They were his pride and joy, his muse, and sometimes his torment.

The curtains were closed in front of him as he took his seat, checking his equipment. It all looked great and he couldn't wait to play. When he was behind his set, all the bullshit disappeared. There were no bills, or dead bodies to dispose of, or vampires you prayed weren't going to get bored with you and rip you apart. No, there was only him and the music.

On the other side of the curtain, he could hear the crowd. They were getting antsy, but Vee and Sarin were taking their sweet ass time.

"Are you ready?" Sarin asked, startling Nic.

He shrugged it off, but he hated when they did that to him.

"Yeah, let's melt some faces." he spun a stick in his fingers.

Sarin smiled and slung her bass around her neck. She looked stunning. She decided to go with a shredded, black t-shirt, that only covered her breasts. She also added a splash of color to her wardrobe for the evening; blood red, leather pants ending with high, combat boots. Her black hair hung around her pale face and red lips.

"Sorry we're late," Vee said, grabbing her guitar. She made a couple of last-minute adjustments. "We were talking with a very interesting young lady," she said, smiling. Her wardrobe seldom changed. Her breasts swung free in the tank top and green hair stood on end.

"Oh, very nice," Nic said, knowing the song and dance. "Hopefully she'll make her way up front and I can get a peek."

Sarin smiled, "Trust me, you'll see her."

From beyond the curtain, the MC made his announcements.

"Alright, fuckers, we have our next act up for ear-splitting enjoyment." He paused, probably reading from a cue card. "From the bowels of Hell, I give you, *A Gift of Death*."

Sarin smiled as the curtains opened.

FOR THE FIRST TIME, Cyril and Nestor saw the vampires in the flesh. Each of them felt a tingle when Sarin spoke. There was something rich and intoxicating about her voice. They knew better, knowing about the glamor a vampire can have.

They didn't move, rather just watched. They watched the crowd stir at the scantily clad lead singer and the guitar player, who they could easily tell wasn't wearing a bra. Yes, they were sexy, but the brothers knew better. A cobra was a beautiful animal until it sunk its fangs into your flesh.

With a couple of brief introductions, the band began their set. The show had finally begun.

SHE WAS BEAUTIFUL. Death wrapped in a cloak of cream-pale skin, black hair, and thick curves.

Cameron couldn't take his eyes off Sarin, as she began speaking, no, yelling to the crowd. His heart fluttered, feeling what he thought love should feel like. He kept his eyes locked on her, wishing he was near her, knowing she was his destiny.

The lights dimmed, the stage going dark. An ominous and slow note began humming from Vee-Exx's guitar. Cameron's body trembled, the music giving him a coating of goosebumps.

Red lights bathed the stage, making the band appear to be covered in blood. Nic began a slow tapping on his symbol, rising with the thrum of the guitar.

Cameron pushed his way through the crowd, who were all staring in anticipation.

A spotlight of white lit up, shining on Sarin. She opened her mouth and began singing.

THE ENERGY of the crowd was intoxicating. It was almost as good as pure, virgin blood, but not quite. Sarin screamed their violent lyrics, the first song in their set was called, *Rape in the Dirt.*

She loved this song and the double bass in the chorus was a crowd-pleaser. It was almost always their opening song. The lyrics flowed from her mouth like honey, if that honey contained razor blades.

The crowd loved it. Black-clothed bodies smashed into each other. Fists, feet, and black hair flew around in a maelstrom of the mosh pit.

Sarin loved it. She loved the chaos of it, the pain some of them felt when a well-aimed fist met teeth or the soft cartilage of the nose. Best of all was the blood. When, and it was always when and never 'if', it was spilled, she relished in it. The surprise and pain were almost erotic, like that person's sex face. The face they'd make when they came into their camper of nightmares as she and Vee pleasured them for the last time in their lives. Pleasure, some of the best, followed by the fiery pain of sharp teeth ripping into flesh. Scaly, almost lupin tongues lapping at lifeblood flowing from opened throats and arteries.

Sarin was getting aroused, which was nothing new. Music made her want to fuck and feed, two of her most favorite things. Both of which she was searching for. Her eyes scanning the crowd, trying to find her next meal.

In the sea of violence, there was one calm spot. Sarin's eyes locked with his. A boy, maybe he could've been in high school, stood still as people banged into him. The chaos around him seemed to be non-existent as he stared up at her. For the moment their eyes locked, Sarin felt a shiver run through her already cold body. Something about him shook her, almost making her miss her next couple of lines.

She broke the momentary gaze, the boy forgotten, and remembered what she was looking for. She found it.

Just on the fringes of the pit stood a woman, no older than 25. She was bobbing her long, bleach-blond hair to the rhythm of the music. She held a red cup high in the air, exposing her smooth, flat midriff.

Sarin watched her, waiting for her to make eye contact.

The woman, lost in her dancing and drink, felt a nudge, an unshakeable feeling. She looked at the band, locking eyes with the lead singer.

Sarin had her. She smiled as Vee-Exx entered a solo. The woman smiled back, raising her cup even higher in a toast. Sarin picked up the lyrics again, all the while wondering what the mystery woman would taste like.

NESTOR DIDN'T CARE for cigarettes, but his brother would indulge from time to time. It was one of Cyril's most healthy addictions and Nestor was almost positive his brother had one, if not multiple STDs. Not that his sex life was any better. He fully planned on having sex with the old, smoked-smelling receptionist at the motel, but she never came. Luckily for her.

Smoking did have its advantages. One, which he was currently exploiting, was the ability to linger outside in the chill night air.

The set of *A Gift of Death* had ended five minutes earlier. Cyril and Nestor pushed their way out of the building, each moist with sweat. They knew there was some time before the band had broken down their equipment and would be heading out. They went back to their car and grabbed a revolver and firebomb.

Huddled and smoking carefully, they stood at the back of the venue watching the black camper.

"How the fuck are we going to do this here?" Cyril asked, his collar pulled up around his neck. He shivered, the cigarette in his mouth, and hands stuffed in his pockets.

Nestor puffed on his but didn't inhale. He watched workers and fans milling around the parking lot, some looking for band members to bombard. The camper was still quiet, but they had to come out sooner than later. He didn't know what they were going to do. An attack in the lot would undoubtedly get them caught. Even if they did succeed, there would be questions, questions neither of them wanted to answer. They couldn't spend their earnings if they were in prison.

"I don't know, but we have to figure something out," Nestor said, bringing the smoke back to his mouth.

The door opened from the back of the venue and there they were. Sarin and Vee carried black guitar cases, which were covered in satanic-looking labels and stickers. Nic, with some help, wheeled out a couple of square cases containing his drums.

Nestor's right hand gripped the butt of his revolver, which was in his hoodie pocket. If it was just as simple as shooting them, he could do it. He was a decent shot and they weren't expecting an attack. At least he hoped they weren't. No, it was much more than that. The beasts needed to be bathed in the holy fire to banish them from the realm of the living.

"Easy," Cyril said, watching his brother shake with tension. "We don't need anyone on to us." He tossed his cigarette butt on the ground and stamped it out. "Come on, let's go to the car and wait." He shivered again, "I'm fucking freezing."

Nestor tossed his cigarette down too, happy to be rid of it. "You're right. Let's warm-up and we'll figure this shit out." He caressed the gun, feeling the oiled steel, cold and slick. Memories of his father, the big gun in his hands, came back. He knew this was in his blood. The vampires would die.

CAMERON LINGERED in the parking lot, waiting for his chance. He didn't have a plan, just like at the mini-mall. He was just going to wing it and let the chips fall where they may.

The night was chilly, but he was sweating. Not only from the body heat of the concert, but from anticipation. Then, he went cold.

The band came walking out carrying their equipment as they headed towards the camper. He watched them all, moving with grace and predatory sleekness. Something else caught his eye; two men watching the band as well.

This wasn't out of the ordinary for men especially, to ogle the two female vampires, but it was the way they looked at them. There was no lust in their eyes, only hatred, and disgust. Cameron knew the look well; it was the only way his mother looked at him. The two men flicked cigarettes on the blacktop and walked away, melting into the shadows of a nearby alley.

A peel of laughter broke the night air.

Cameron looked back near the camper. Vee and Sarin were standing outside talking with a young, blond woman. She was wearing a black t-shirt and had her arms crossed under her breasts. Cameron felt a pang of jealousy as Sarin laughed at something the woman said. Vee-Exx didn't do much talking, just smiling and staring at the woman. Sarin backed up and opened the door of the camper. Red light poured from the inside as she stepped in, holding her hand out.

The woman looked around as if trying to find a friend or maybe a way out, but when she locked eyes with the vampire again, her fate was sealed.

Cameron was on the verge of tears. It should've been him in the camper with them, not some skank.

Slowly, the camper began to move out of the parking lot.

Cameron wiped his face and jogged back to his car. This was his destiny and he wouldn't let it pass him by.

"So, Christie, did you like the show?" Sarin asked, handing the woman a drink.

Christie took the cup. She didn't want to drink, as she was pretty drunk, but didn't want to be rude. Besides, there was something about the lead singer that was making her swoon.

"I loved it," Christie said, sipping. She grimaced at the bitter tang of alcohol. "Damn, that's strong," she said, holding the cup in the air as if Sarin could see through the red plastic.

Vee, who was seated at the table, laughed. "Yeah, she doesn't know when enough is enough." She looked at Sarin, who was still eyeing the young woman.

"Oh, yes, I do love a good strong drink. It just makes things so much better. Don't you agree, Christie?" Sarin asked, willing the woman to drink.

Christie took another sip, the drink was not nearly as bitter, then a gulp. "Yeah," she said, the cup to her face, "it lubes the gears." Her voice echoed in the cup before she put it down.

Sarin laughed. "In this camper, there's no need for lube." She looked at Vee, "Right, Vee?"

Vee stood and slid in next to Christie, who had to shuffle over so as not to be sat on. "That's right," Vee said, her fingers playing with Christie's chemically enhanced hair.

Christie drank, trying to hide her embarrassment. She never, ever had any lesbian thoughts, in fact, she thought it was gross when guys would go down on her. But this was different. There was something about the two women in front of her making her slick with lust. The twin barbells pierced through her nipples ached with anticipation. They hummed, her body visualizing each woman gently biting her breasts, teasing the rods of steel with sharp teeth.

Vee reached over, taking the cup from Christie's hand. Her mouth was near the woman's neck; eyes glued to the throb of her arteries and veins.

Vee kissed her, gently on her collarbone, eliciting a deep moan.

Christie wasn't used to the smoothness of a woman's mouth and cheek on her skin. It was usually a rough, stubbly face pecking away. It was heavenly, even though the other woman's lips were ice cold.

Vee reached under the table and began rubbing Christie's thighs.

Christie's eyes were closed, her body warming with electric pleasure. She ran her fingers through Vee's short hair, pulling her face harder into her neck. She could feel movement and part of her knew Sarin was about to join in. She opened her eyes and saw Sarin sitting across from her.

"Let's take this into the bedroom," she said, leaning across, licking Christie's lips. "Then I can taste your other lips as well."

The camper bounced, Nic guiding it off-road to an old parking area for fishing access. He glanced over his shoulder as Vee and Sarin led the doomed woman into the bedroom. He watched the road, and tried to pay attention to the goings-on in the back of the camper. He never noticed the two vehicles in tow.

CYRIL AND NESTOR sat parked with their lights off. The camper was about 100 feet away, but still visible by the moonlight.

They coasted in, with their vehicle dark, praying they didn't get spotted. The moon blessed them with just enough light to see, following the taillights of the camper.

Nestor looked at Cyril. He could tell his brother was itching for a smoke but knew better. The scent or sight of the cigarette could spell death for them both.

"Are you ready?" Nestor asked, opening the cylinder of his revolver. He touched each shell, silently saying a prayer. The holy water infused firebomb was in a small pouch on his belt.

Cyril checked his gun and looked at his brother. "Yes," He snapped the cylinder closed. "Let's fucking do this."

CAMERON FOLLOWED THE CAR. He was the last in the procession of vehicles. At least he hoped he was.

When the camper turned off the road and into a dirt trail, Cameron's heart began to race. This was it. The end was coming and he felt it in his bones. He didn't know what the involvement of the other car was, but the sheer fact they drove with their lights off, parked far away, and had been eyeing the band, didn't give Cameron hope. It was doubtful they were there to ask about buying a vacuum or time-share.

The two men got out of their car, each with something in their hands. Guns. Each man carried an unholstered, heavy revolver. Even from the distance Cameron was, he knew the glint of gunmetal in the moonlight. Nothing good could come from them. They were threatening his future, something Cameron couldn't let happen.

He pulled his father's .45 from his waistband and checked the chamber. It was still loaded. He cocked the hammer back and thumbed off the safety. By the silvery light of the moon, he got out of the car, not bothering to close the door.

BLOOD-CURDLING SCREAMS CAME from the bedroom.

Vee ripped into Christie's neck but failed to take her vocal cords on the first bite. Hot, coppery, and nourishing blood flooded her salivating mouth. Jagged, sharp teeth tore through living flesh like it was nothing, melting in her mouth. Vee moaned, almost orgasmically as she fed.

The nude woman bucked and clawed at the vampire attached to her neck, but her fists might as well have been cotton. If Christie was able to look down, she would've seen one of her breasts was gone. What remained was a tattered flap of skin and a few yellowish lumps of fat. Her breast had landed against the wall, a Rorschach print where it struck.

Sarin, in her lust and hunger, ripped it free moments before her teeth sunk into Christie's thigh. She was so caught up in the heady scent of the woman's vagina and the rushing of the blood in her femoral artery, she couldn't help herself. She tore off the smooth, creamy breast with demonic claws.

Vee saw the attack coming but wasn't ready. Sarin made that choice for her when she ripped Christie's breast off and tore into her thigh. Vee's bite was awry, thus missing the vocal cords. It didn't matter, Nic had done a great job finding them a remote place to not only feed but dispose of the corpse.

The fight was out of Christie as her body drifted into shock, just before the cold embrace of death.

———

THE CAMPER ROCKED as Vee and Sarin fed.

Nic knew the process all too well. After they fed, they would lick and bite each other, offering their bodies to one another for their carnal desires. Once they both had their fill, they'd summon him. He knew he had some time to kill until they were ready. He grabbed his smokes and gun and got out of the camper.

He put the gun in the small of his back and lit a cigarette. He took out his cell phone and began scrolling. The camper stopped rocking and he could hear suckling noises. Something else caught his attention; another sound.

Footsteps.

Nic looked up from his phone, his night vision compromised from the bright screen.

Two men stood in front of him, each with a revolver pointed at his head.

"Don't fucking move," one of them said. His hand was steady.

Nic kept his hands near his waist, wanting to raise them in the air. This was clearly a robbery and he didn't need his gun. There was something far more lethal inside the camper.

"Be cool, fellas," Nic said, swallowing hard. His finger started to burn when he realized he still held a smoldering cigarette. "Take what you want, ok. There's a ton of stuff inside and all our equipment is on the back of the camper." Nic said, a little louder, hoping Vee and Sarin would make a guest appearance, ending this bullshit.

NESTOR SMILED. This guy, Nic, thought this was a robbery.

"We're not here for your shit, dickhead. We're here for them," he said, gesturing towards the camper with his head. "Cyril, torch it."

Cyril looked at his brother. They'd both seen the young blond woman go into the camper. There was a chance she was still alive.

"The girl?" Cyril asked, his barrel dipping lower. He looked at his brother from the corner of his eye.

"Fuck her," Nestor growled. "She's probably dead anyway. Besides, we were paid for a job, not to be heroes."

On cue, a loud thump came from inside the camper.

NIC WAS IN PANIC MODE. These guys, who he foolishly mistook for robbers, were fucking vampire hunters. Their guns, which were just as lethal to him, would do some damage to Vee and Sarin. He couldn't help but notice the glass bottles full of liquid on their hips. If they came out thinking this was an easy fight, the two men would surely kill them. He needed a moment to act. His gun skills weren't the best, but if he got a chance, he'd draw on them.

From inside the camper came a loud thump.

The two men looked.

Nic drew his gun.

CYRIL WATCHED it in slow motion. His and Nestor's eyes came off target for just a fraction of a second and it was all Nic needed.

In a split second, he had a gun in his hand and raised it. A shower of sparks and flame erupted from the muzzle of the gun aimed right at Cyril.

Cyril pulled the trigger on his revolver, the bark muffled in his heightened state. A burst of muzzle flash lit the dark forest and something ripped the air from his lungs. He was falling and couldn't catch his breath. Nestor's gun fired and then he was standing over Cyril, his face starting to fade.

Cyril felt coldness wash over him and then...it went black.

NIC KNEW he was going to die when he saw the big revolver fire. Flame nearly a-foot-long shot from the barrel. The heavy slug struck just above his belly button. The bullet traveled through, the hollow point filling with tissue, blood, and organs. It opened up inside of him, blooming like a flower of death as it impacted his spine. His legs went numb, dropping him to the ground in a heap.

A second shot rang out, this one hitting him in his useless legs. For a second, he was thankful for his paralysis.

The man still standing looked down on the other one, who was fading fast. Nic took solace knowing he killed at least one of them.

He was cold, his blood pooled around him, soaking his clothes. Nic shuddered when he saw the man pull the glass bottle and lighter from his side.

VEE AND SARIN HEARD NIC talking outside, but figured he was on the phone. Their lust and hunger for each other's blood-drenched bodies blocked everything else out.

Until the gunfire.

Sarin was laying on the bed, using the corpse of Christie as a pillow. She watched Vee lovingly eat her out for the second time. Soon, she'd need Nic to come in and put the icing on the cake.

"What the fuck?" Vee said, looking towards the blacked-out windows as gunfire erupted. She stood, her chin wet with blood and vaginal fluid. She reached out to move the black cover from the windows.

The firebomb shattered the thin glass and hit her square in the chest. It burst against her nude flesh, the holy fire covering her.

Vee screamed, her hair melting almost instantly. The fire

changed as it tasted corrupted flesh, turning from orange flame, to white and blue. The cleansing inferno made short work of her, and began to spread, seeking Sarin's dead flesh.

Sarin knew she was in trouble and had only one option. She dove at the other window, praying she'd fit through it.

Her nude body hit the glass and metal frame, taking it out with her. She rolled to the ground, landing at the feet of a man.

A man with a large gun pointed at her.

She could smell the stink of the vampire hunter as he sneered. Her fangs were out and if she had but a moment, she'd kill him. At least she'd go out in her true form.

Another gunshot erupted from the shadows.

CAMERON HAD NEVER SHOT a person before and didn't know if he even could. Maybe except some of the kids at school. He was certain he could kill them with extreme prejudice.

When his father's gun bucked in his hands and he saw the man with the revolver turn, he knew he could kill...if he didn't die first.

Cameron saw the man's leg crumple, the big .45 caliber bullet doing damage as it blew through flesh and bone. That wasn't enough to kill, at least right away.

The man was aiming at him now and Cameron tried to find his sights, but couldn't. All he could see was the black maw of the revolver pointed at him. He pressed the trigger, just as the revolver fired.

His second shot was true, hitting the man just below the right eye, taking a fist-size chunk of his skull and brain as it exited.

Cameron collapsed, burning pain in his gut. He put his hands to his belly, the gun forgotten. Black blood gushed through his fingers. Pain like he'd never felt washed over him.

He'd gotten his wish; he was dying. He coughed, tasting the blood on his lips.

Sarin was coming towards him. She was nude. Her body was tinted brown and red with blood.

Cameron looked up at her, forcing a smile. He was fading, the edges of his vision going dark.

Sarin smiled back with a mouthful of fangs.

A GIFT OF DEATH

THE AIR WAS full of teenage smells. Cheap booze, weed smoke, nervous sweat, and cologne.

To Pat, these were smells of comfort, of his little kingdom of school.

The flames of the bonfire lit up the clearing in the woods. There was no official name for it, but the clearing had been used for generations by high school kids to throw parties. It was deep enough into the woods the cops didn't bother with them, but close enough to town it wasn't an inconvenience.

Pat drank from a cup of beer. He was eyeing Tara, who was with a small group of girls on the other side of the fire. After the prank they played on Cameron, Pat and Tara began talking. It started innocently, just him trying his best to get her to send him legit nudes. She turned him down, but there was something about his asshole-ish charm that drove her wild.

"You gonna hit that?" Tyler asked, walking up next to Pat, his beer in hand.

Pat looked at his buddy and smiled. "I didn't bring a tent and rubbers for nothing," he shook his friend's hand in a way that only douchebags do.

"My man," Tyler said, sipping from his beer. "Yeah, I'm hoping Marley will give me a blowjob later." He drank again. "She's on the rag, or else I'm pretty sure we'd be fucking. But I'll settle for a good BJ."

"Yeah, I heard she's pretty good," Pat smiled at his friend. He hadn't heard, he knew for a fact. Last week she blew him after school. Very random and very much appreciated.

"Holy shit!" Someone said near the fire. "What the fuck are you doing here?"

Pat looked past his friend and into the crowd of other kids. They were all starting to huddle around someone, but Pat couldn't see.

"Let me through," he said, pushing people out of the way. After all, he was the king and they were his subjects. Pat stopped, standing face to face with Cameron.

He laughed. "What the fuck are you doing here?" He asked the other boy.

It had been a week since Cameron's dick pic went viral. No one had seen him and the whole school thought he'd killed himself and was rotting in that shithole apartment.

"We thought, no hoped, you'd killed yourself," Pat said, holding his arms wide, gesturing to the laughing crowd around him.

Tara stayed back, watching from a distance. Something moved in the dark woods behind her, but she couldn't see.

"Anyway," Pat said, stepping up chest to chest with Cameron, "this is a private party." He looked him up and down. "No cheese dicks allowed." The group laughed again, but some didn't. Cameron's calm was eerie.

Cameron smiled. "I'll be gone soon, but I have a gift for you," he started laughing.

Others started laughing too, but not out of humor, but out of nervousness. The air felt heavy, pressing on them. It was as if a storm was getting ready to unleash.

"You don't have anything I could want," Pat said, his nose almost touching Cameron's.

"Oh, I don't know about that," Cameron said, smelling the beer on Pat's breath. "There," he pointed to Tara, who was standing by herself at the fire.

They all turned, looking at Tara. She, not knowing what they were looking at, turned around, peering into the gloom.

Sarin burst from the shadows. Her mouth was wide with razor-sharp teeth. Her clawed thumbs found Tara's soft eyeballs. She plunged them in, feeling the rewarding pop as the membrane burst.

Tara screamed for a second before her throat was ripped out in a shower of gore.

The crowd screamed and began to run, as Sarin dropped Tara's corpse and grabbed another girl by her ponytail. Sarin used her claws to pull her windpipe out before she bit her face off. Half of the girl's tongue lolled from her mangled face. The vampire wasn't concerned about feeding at the moment. No, she wanted to kill, and kill she did.

Pat stood frozen, watching the woman rip his friends apart. He'd forgotten about Cameron standing in front of him. He turned and looked into the dead, black eyes of the boy he so loved to torment. His bowels and bladder voiding.

Cameron took in the fear-filled smell of piss and shit.

He smiled at his bully. With a mouthful of fangs.

ABOUT THE AUTHOR

Daniel J. Volpe is an author of extreme horror and splatterpunk.

His love for horror started at a young age when his grandfather unwittingly rented him "A Nightmare on Elm Street."

Daniel has published some of his stories with Raven's Inn Press, Sirens Call Publications, Twisted Tales, Exiles Literary Magazine, Literati Publications and has self published.

In November of 2020, he published the splatterpunk novella, BILLY SILVER, which has received praise from peers and readers alike. He can be found on Facebook @ Daniel J. Volpe, Instagram @ dj_volpe_horror, Twitter DJVolpehorror and online at https://danielvolpe909.wixsite.com/danieljvolpehorror

ABOUT THE EDITOR / PUBLISHER

Dawn Shea is an author and half of the publishing team over at
D&T Publishing. She lives with her family in Mississippi.
Always an avid horror lover, she has moved forward with her
dreams of writing and publishing those things she loves so
much.

D.&T Previously published material:
    ABC's of Terror
    After the Kool-Aid is Gone

Follow her author page on Amazon for all publications she is
featured in.
    Follow D&T Publishing at the following locations:
    Website
    Facebook: Page / Group
    Or email us here: dandtpublishing20@gmail.com

Produced by D&T Publishing LLC

Collected by Dawn Ellis Shea

Formatting by J.Z. Foster

Corinth, MS

A Gift of Death

Printed in Great Britain
by Amazon

28015822R00076